RUBÉN MENDOZA

LOTERÍA
and other stories

gallo catchetón books

"Second Thoughts" and "9th of October" (as "to die for") originally appeared in *Con Safos* magazine.

First gallo catchetón books edition published 1996

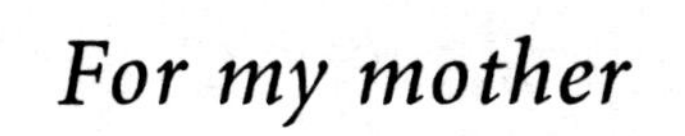
For my mother

Contents

L O T E R Í A

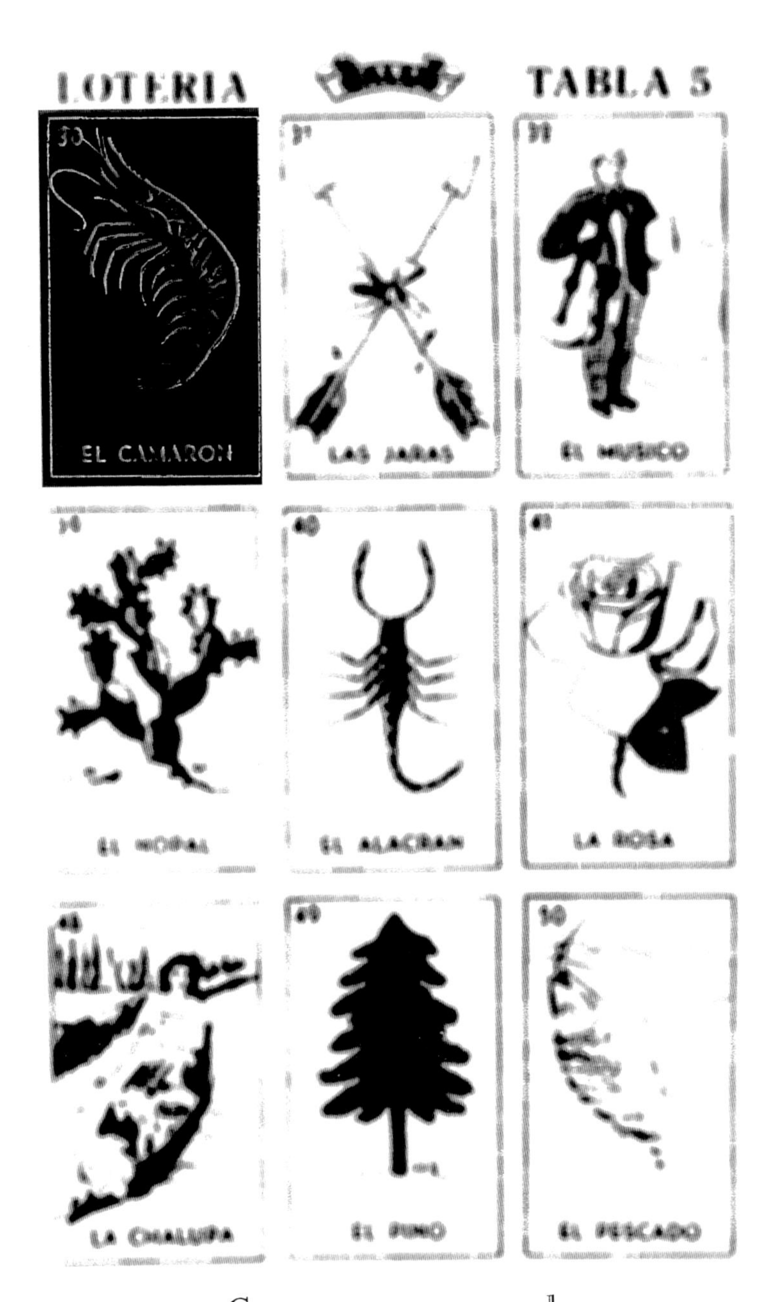

Camarón que se duerme,
se lo lleva la corriente.

Second Thoughts

He started, as usual, by noticing his feet. Right away he noticed, at the bottom of his left foot, inside his sock, a small pebble, or a sliver of a toenail perhaps, which poked into his sole each time he wiggled his foot. He dreaded the thought of stepping down on this foot, because he knew he would not be able to remove the thing which poked at him. So he just wriggled his toes and scrunched his muscles to try to shift the thing to a more comfortable position.

There was also something else nagging at him, some thought he could not yet grasp. It was something he was forgetting maybe, some feeling or idea that shivered there on the edge of his consciousness like an elusive shadow he was not sure he'd seen. It would come to him, though. He was certain.

He worked his way up his legs. The ankles and knees felt more stiff and rigid than usual. He tried bending them, but this brought dull pain and a tingling sensation at the base of his spine, both of which subsided when he gave up efforts to move. He needed his pain-killers if he wanted to make it to the store to pick up some cucumbers and shrimp. He'd promised her he would make her some of his famous cocteles campechanos. Crab, avocado, oysters, tomatoes, clams, onions, cilantro, abulón, cucumbers, and shrimp. Every Sunday evening for years now he'd made enough for the two of them to enjoy while the sun went down.

But this week the cocteles might have to wait, maybe until tomorrow. He continued up his thighs to his groin. His thighs were numb, and his groin felt like some kind of black void of un-feeling. The urge to fornicate had begun to subside years ago with his youth, but this was different. It felt now as though nothing were there, as though there never had been. In a way, he felt a strange relief in this. He reached for his penis to make sure it was still there, but then thought better of it. There was no rush. It could wait.

He noticed next his stomach and his intestines, which no longer grumbled with the gastrointestinal difficulties of the past few years. He sighed in relief at this merciful, if temporary respite, and moved up to his chest. His heart was very quiet, and his lungs felt somehow cleaned of the layers of blackness years of smoking had coated them with. He seemed to breath easier now, and he attributed this to the dryness of the room.

The shadow still shivered there in his mind, but suddenly he noticed that the pain in his legs was gone, even when he moved them. He stretched out his fingers and marveled at the ease with which he created two wrinkled fists at his sides. The arthritis had decided to leave him today, and he smiled. Again, he attributed this to the climate.

Up his neck to his face...he felt his cheeks, clean-shaven and sticky, perhaps with sweat. He rolled his eyes around and ground his teeth, then licked the front of his top row of teeth. They were a little dirty-he had not brushed since...since...for quite a while, but that also could wait a bit longer.

Finally, he came to his brain. He could feel it working there in the darkness, sending and receiving eletro-chemical signals through synapses and neurotransmitters which branched out to every point in his body. One plus one equals two, he thought, just to make sure everything was working okay. Two and two is five, he thought, just for fun. He smiled.

Now he could turn his attention outside himself. Still, that thing nagged at him. But he knew he would remember it in time, and he listened around him. A voice spoke in solemn tones in another room close by. He thought he heard his name mentioned, and there were other familiar things in what the voice said, but he couldn't quite grasp them. Now that the pain in his legs was gone, he was thinking again about going to the market for some cucumbers and fresh shrimp. He'd promised her he would make it for her.

He heard music. It was sad: an organ, and a voice which sang in Spanish above the instrument. He could smell a strange chemical smell, something familiar–formaldehyde, perhaps, and that shimmering idea almost crystallized as he struggled to hold it within the smell. But then he smelled her.

In all the years he'd known her, she'd always worn a light floral scent which mixed well with the smells of her body. He smelled it now and smiled. For some reason, it reminded him of that evening above Monument Valley.

At the time, the moment had passed almost completely unnoticed and forgotten like so many others in youth-probably lasting no more than a second. Yet now he grasped at it desperately as her smell filled his lungs because he knew it had something to do with what he was supposed to remember. Her smell was like orchids, and as it filled him, he closed his eyes and thought about that evening.

They were young, and he remembered, as they sat against each other on a wall overlooking the valley, how in love they'd been. They'd watched the setting desert sun paint the valley dark red as the warm early evening wind kissed them both and lulled them into silence. Her hair smelled like orchids and warm rain, and he remembered the heat of her body pressing up against his.

Even at that age, he had known for quite some time already that there was no God. And yet here, in this valley, he'd felt something far greater than himself, some ineffable presence beyond himself which brought him close to tears, and close to something he knew he might never grasp. It threatened to swallow him up, and he remembered how his breath had escaped his lungs as that thing held him in its power, pushing him and pushing him with its sheer immensity until it reached a deafening point and he'd turned suddenly and buried his face into her neck in some strange mixture of desperate fear and exultation. Her smell of orchids and warm rain had washed over him and saved him. Afterwards, that moment above the valley was forever wed, through mysterious synaptic connections and pathways he would never understand, to the smells of her body and perfume.

And now as he thought about that moment, he suddenly realized what he had been feeling as he looked out at that valley so many years ago, and what he had been trying all his life to remember and understand. That same presence was here with him again, pushing, pushing, pushing until the idea finally crystallized in his brain, and it was so clear to him now he could no longer ignore it. It was so clear, and he wanted, needed, desperately to tell her, before it was too late.

Honey, he tried to whisper. He could tell she was very near. *Honey, listen to me. That time at Monument Valley, when we were young, on the way to New Orleans, remember? Honey, it wasn't the valley, or the wind, or your perfume. It was inside me. The...the valley was just a valley, and the wind was just wind, and your smell...your smell was just your smell. And the valley, and the wind, and your smell, will always be there.*

But at that moment, they were everything. Everything. Do you understand? For that second, they were everything because I made them everything. I made the valley beautiful. I made the wind sublime. I made your smell ecstatic. And in return, they made me real, for just a second, because these feelings, and the beauty, and the ecstasy, all came from inside of me- and from nowhere else. They were all things that came from inside me and from nowhere else.

Just for a second, baby, I was real-for that short second, I was real, and that's all I could ever really hope for...but that's enough...because it made me human, and that's enough. That's what makes us, honey. Do you understand?

She was nodding, and he knew somehow she'd heard. He had remembered, and she heard him.

I just need some cucumbers and shrimp, and she nodded. *I love you*, and still she nodded. He breathed a sigh of relief and felt his body relax. He could rest; she knew. She understood.

He smiled, and then-suddenly-another second began. He started, as usual, by noticing his feet.

El farol de enamorados.

Green Moons

moon: (moon) *n* 1. The natural satellite of Earth, approx. 221,600 miles at perigee and 252,950 miles at apogee, and having a mean diameter of 2,160 miles, mass approx. one eightieth that of Earth, and an average period of revolution around Earth of 29 days 12 hours 44 minutes.-*The American Heritage Dictionary, Third Edition*

la luna: "El farol de enamorados." -*Lotería, Pasatiempos Gallo de Don Clemente*

When we fall asleep together, she is the picture of feline grace and affection, curling up against my body, pressing her comfortable warmth into mine, and holding me around her like another of her blankets. But there are nights I stay up very late, writing, or watching T.V., or just thinking there in the dark when my mind refuses to shut off. On these nights, when I crawl cold into bed where she has been sleeping for quite some time already-say, a few hours or so-I've noticed that she has become a somewhat different character.

After a few hours of sleep, her body takes on a decidedly harsher persona, like some kind of unconscious automaton. The movements are jerky and rough-a quick scratching hand falls back carelessly from her scalp to the pillow with a crude thud, a restless leg flops over my hip and shakes the bed, then pulls back roughly, the toenails scraping invisible tracks along my leg, or her head turns away from my chest with loud, annoyed exhalations as she pulls the covers over her body and away from me.

Sometimes I try to slip an arm beneath her unyielding head. It's all a wasted effort though, because even if I succeed, I must then lie next to this body which cries out with each unconscious action and breath to get away from me. And it's not just the movement, either; her stillness is just as uncomfortable and unyielding, rejecting in its very perfection.

The breathing bothers me too. It is not the graceful, even, deep breathing of the classic beauty in repose, nor is it the light, peaceful undulation of air moving in and out of lungs and the resulting, more aesthetically pleasing rise and fall of the fair maiden's breast as her lover looks on, enraptured. No, the breathing here is asthmatic: short, harsh, at times spasmodic, and almost always, frightening. It's an impatient storm, annoyed with the darkness of dreams, or perhaps with the precious time lost in unconsciousness. Or maybe, it's the body pressing up next to her which causes her limbs and internal organs to recoil this way.

And I wonder if this is how I am when I enter my own world of sleep. Am I as cold? Am I as annoyed and angered at having my unconsciousness disturbed by the presumptuousness of someone else's? And when we are both asleep, do we grope at each other with equally harsh, unconscious motions as our worlds collide, pushing fiercely at each other until our respective sides of the bed have been successfully claimed, staked out, and defended? How many silent battles do we wage throughout the night? How many kingdoms are won and lost? How many wars conceded?

She's turned away from me and I stare at her shoulder, soft green in the flickering glow of a VCR's digital display. No, it's just soft green because I say so-or rather, because you imagine it is green when I say it-or at least, that was the plan. There is really no VCR and, therefore, no digital display, and no green light, but it doesn't matter really where the greenness comes from. There is just her green shoulder glowing there like Kryptonite, or, like radiation in some late-night, post-apocalyptic science fiction B-film, or, like the digital numbers of a VCR display. Take your pick.

Or maybe it's not green at all, but blue, blue like a seagull tossed about in the sharp crosswinds of a clear sky above the Pacific Ocean, or blue like the dull, smoky shine of a sweaty jazz musician's wingtip shoes, or blue, like an abnormally large, ripe, biologically-altered tomato.

No, it (her shoulder) is green after all. Green like some strange alien landscape, a gentle, peaceful meadow rising and falling on some distant world, sloping gracefully down to the shadows of her neck. And there, an ancient, dry lake bed where alien lovers once swam naked, protected beneath the soft canopy of their goddess' dark hair, thousands and thousands of years ago.

There are millions of these ancient, alien lovers, swimming

and sliding their warm underwater bodies against one another in silent, orgiastic ecstasy, then drying off entwined in the rolling green meadows which press gently up against the dark lake. They are lovers who play in darkness; they are lovers who dance naked in the warm light of a green moon, caressing one another in its soft glow, kissing one another, licking one another with a million million silvery tongues, tenderly, quietly.

I reach out and lay my palm gently on her shoulder, and this time the flesh is soft, compliant and welcoming beneath my touch, and tingling with the electricity of a million atoms and molecules brushing, colliding, gliding lithely past and over and through one another, and jumping from my skin to hers, and hers to mine. With delicate fingertips, I trace the curve of her arm down to her hand, where I play with all seven elegant fingers, then down to one of her smooth, tan, statuesque legs, then to another, and then another, and another, and then up to the wiry, swampy forest of her pubis, where I draw zig-zagging lines that twist and turn their way out in myriad, endless branchings until the forest finally recedes mercifully into softer and softer meadows of light-colored down which make forbidden, naughty borders with one of her many warm, hidden, completely smooth bellies. Finally, my fingers find her forty-seven large, full, environmentally-safe, pesticide-free, and perfectly-shaped, golden breasts.

I cannot see them...I cannot see beyond...I cannot see them beyond. I cannot see them beyond her shoulder, but their softness and warmth fill me, and just the idea that they are there is enough to ensure that they really are. I...I...She...no, I...cup two of them in her hand, and feel my...her...my nipple press comfortably against his palm, then I smile and let his body relax as she presses her back and her stomach into me. He closes my eyes and I watch your shoulder glowing soft and green and rolling gently there in the dark, an endless, agitated whisper of flesh and bone and warm, coursing, green blood, and I know, at least for now, that there will be no more battles between us, between them. My drowsy eyes close and feign sleep, until finally I am dancing and writhing naked there in her meadow, again, with human-alien lovers, on strange, ancient worlds, in the silent glow of green moons.

Este mundo es una bola
y nosotros un bolón.

TRAFFIC

I had told Nanette I would pick her up at 7:30. It was already 7:23. She had just moved into a new condominium in the Hollywood hills, and I had to take Sunset to get there. I knew she would probably be angry with me for making her wait, but I really couldn't decide if this worried me or not, and as I began to speed through a yellow light at Highland Avenue, something caught my eye on my left-hand side and I slowed to a stop to let the light turn red.

On the sidewalk in front of Rally's Burgers, I watched a huge, floppy king-sized mattress move toward the intersection. The mattress turned to move into the crosswalk, and the two men carrying it came into view. The mattress had no handles, and the taller of the two men, a hunch-backed white guy, kept dropping his end of it. Every time he did this, the other, a short black man, would yell at him. I watched while they crossed the street in front of me. My window was halfway down, and as they came closer, I listened.

"Hold it up, you're getting it wet," the black guy said. The street was still slick and soaked from an earlier rainstorm, and I could see that the corner of the mattress that kept getting dropped was indeed becoming more and more visibly wet. A dark stain of dirty water was spreading there.

"I can't hold it up any more. My hands hurt," the white guy said. Again, the mattress slipped out of his hands to the ground and he scrambled to pick it up by its edges. As they came closer, I could see that the mattress was in a very sorry state. It had brown and yellow stains, holes with yellowish stuffing and rusted springs poking out, and rips and tears all along the edges. It was a thin, worn mattress, the kind you find in cheap motels with bent, burned spoons and used hypodermic needles hidden underneath.

When they were right in front of me, the white guy with the hurting hands let the mattress fall and twist onto the hood of my car. He held his left wrist in his right hand, then his right wrist in his left hand, alternating nervously every few seconds, and I could see tears streaming down his face. He looked dazed, and I realized he was stoned.

"Pick it up, asshole," the black guy said, and his big eyes darted quickly in my direction as the cross-traffic light turned yellow and my light prepared to turn green.

"I can't, Eddie. My hands hurt." In my headlights I could see now that he was very dirty, with long matted hair, soiled, torn pants, and a tattered, stained pink bathrobe which came down to his knees. He had a scraggly beard. Holding his raw, red hands out in front of him and watching Eddie with glazed eyes, he looked like a crucified Jesus.

The black guy, Eddie, was also dirty. He wore endless layers of filthy shirts, jackets, polyester pants, aerobic leggings, knit sweaters, multi-colored scarves, and torn fishnet stockings. He began yelling at the Jesus guy again as my light turned green. "C'mon man, help me move this thing," he said, but the Jesus guy just stood there and stared at the mattress on my hood, holding out his hands. The cars behind me began to honk, then started pulling into the lane next to mine to pass us. As they drove by, I could hear them yelling at us. I turned on my hazard lights and wondered what to do.

I stuck my head out the window and said, "Hey, c'mon, get your mattress off my car," and Eddie said, "Yeah, c'mon asshole, let's go," as he pushed the Jesus guy's shoulder. I thought maybe he was afraid I would run them over or something, and I gunned my engine lightly.

"But my hands hurt, Eddie," the Jesus guy said. He did not move, even when Eddie pushed him, but instead just stood there in front of my car, staring at the mattress and the headlights like a catatonic deer.

"Shit! You prick!" Eddie said. "Man, this was your stupid idea, now I gotta carry this shit by myself." Eddie began pulling on the mattress and trying to lift it. It slid off the hood and flat onto the wet ground in front of my car, then lay there like some uncooperative, rotting animal carcass that refused to be moved. He kept trying to pick it up, but it was too high for him to hold up off the ground without the help of his taller friend. Finally, I got out of my car and walked over to him. The Jesus guy had wandered off toward Hollywood High School, still holding his wrists and crying.

"Here, let me help you get this onto the sidewalk," I said, but Eddie just stood there.

"What for?" he said. "I can't take it anywhere by myself. I'll have to leave it there."

"Well, I'm sorry, but it's blocking the street," I said, as

people continued to pass, staring out their windows and yelling obscenities at us.

"Listen," he said, grabbing hold of my sleeve and leaning forward so I could see his black, rotting teeth. "Help me out, man. We were taking this just up the street here behind the gas station on Franklin so we could have something to sleep on, you know? We could put it on top of your car and just drive it up there. It won't even take five minutes. You don't know what this would mean to me."

I considered helping him out. It really wouldn't be too much trouble, and it was raining. I mean, it wasn't like he was asking for money to buy drugs or something. He just wanted something comfortable to sleep on. It was a chance to actually, really help. But I could smell the alcohol and body odor on him, and I began to imagine him sitting in my newly washed car, the mattress on the roof, his smell seeping comfortably into the fabric of my seats and then lingering there for weeks. I had a date to pick up, and I was already late.

"No, I don't think so," I said. "Here, I'll put it on the sidewalk for you, but you're on your own after that." I started pulling the mattress toward the sidewalk. The edges rubbed my fingertips and made them feel raw as I tried to get some kind of grip on the mattress. I could smell urine and sex on it. I tried to hold it away from my clothes, and this made it even harder to move. Eddie just stood there, scowling, shaking his head, and watching me drag the mattress off the street.

"White bastard," he said, as I lifted the edge onto the sidewalk corner. There was a Middle Eastern restaurant in the strip mall there. Above the restaurant was a green neon sign that made the mattress glow like Kryptonite in a sick lime-green color. "Fuck you," he said in a rough, husky voice. I didn't look up at him. I let the mattress fall to the sidewalk and rubbed my burning hands on my pants, then sniffed them quickly, hoping he wouldn't notice. He let out a disgusted grunt.

It began to rain again, lightly, as I walked back to my car. He stood on the corner next to the Kryptonite mattress, staring at me, and I could feel his eyes on my back as I walked in front of my headlights. My neck was burning, and my shirt felt damp and sticky under my arms. I got into my car and shut the door, and as I began to drive off, out of the corner of my eye, I could see him walking away up Highland Avenue, cursing to himself, maybe looking for the Jesus guy, the mattress left hanging partly off the curb as the rain began to fall harder.

Later, when I picked up Nanette, she was angry that I had taken so long. I said, "I'm sorry, but I ran into some traffic on Sunset," and we went out for sushi and plum wine.

El que espera,
desespera.

Mi Amor

I am so tired, mi amor. I have watched for two thousand years with these blind walnut eyes. I have stood in this desert and felt the wind blow souls through these empty eyes while I nourished this tree, nourished its solitary pear and watched it grow, watched it change a million colors, hanging heavier and heavier with each dying sun. I think it is ready, mi 'jito, and I think I am ready. I have waited. I am ready, mi vida. I have waited, and I. I am...

waiting for him in Nogales, I watched two thousand years march by. In Nogales there are no pears. The sand and rocks and clay blow through me like whispers of the dead. There are scorpions and tarantulas and nopales, but I have never seen a single pear in this gray desert. But he told me about them, mi 'jo. He held me in the shadowy mountains of his arms and stroked my long black hair naked under the heavy desert stars and told me don't worry, mi amor. He told me there are gold pears, perfect gold pears that hang heavy like rich, ripe breasts and pull the branches to the very earth with their weight. And their taste. Their taste is...the taste is pure gold, sweet, soft-the taste dissolves in your sigh, mi amor. And he whispered to me that the greatest secret is inside. Hijo, he told me there are some that have perfect white pearls growing inside them. Imagine, perfect pears growing perfect pearls. Perfect pearls and perfect pears. Perfect. Pearls and. Pearls and perfect...

pears will save us, I said to him. Go to California and find them, mi amor, and we will wait here for you. I will wait here while this pearl grows inside of me. Go, mi amor. Step over mountains with your heavy black boots, scoop whole bundles of trees into your arms like glowing gold match sticks and blow them to me on the wind of your kiss. Send me your golden pears with their white pearls. I will sing the songs of golden pears, I will sing of you to our son, I will wait with him in my womb and then in my arms for the pears to pour down on us in showers of gold ashes from the wind of your love. We will wait for you here in Nogales. We will wait for you. We will wait. We will. Wait. Wait for...

you will take me inside now, no? take your mama's pale skinny arm and lead her through her blind darkness and put her in bed. You will brush my tangled white hair and we will sing, hijo. Together, we will wait for him and sing the songs of golden pears, and you will watch me nod my tired head until I fall asleep, no? Until I stop my singing. Until I. You will watch. I. You will...

watch the setting desert sun paint the rocks blood red. Please, let me watch my dying sun paint this pear a million shades of gold, no? Please, and then I will go in. Then we can go, okay? Please wait for me, mi amor. I think my pear is almost ready. I am almost ready. I can see it there, hanging heavy to the ground just like he said, hanging just like he said they do in California. Oh mi 'jito, it's so beautiful. I wish you could see my pear. Inside I can see the pearl just like he said, glowing white hot through the gold skin. It blinds me. It calls out to me with its magic. It calls out my name and invites me. It's so warm and comfortable. It calls. It waits. It. Calls out. Out to...

mi amor, oh I have waited so long for you to bring me my pear, so long. I have waited two thousand years for my pear, but I never gave up. I knew you would come for me. I knew you would come back to me, shaking the mud from your thick black boots and swinging tornadoes with your heavy mountain arms. I knew. I knew you. I knew you would...

come to me, please. Bring me my pear and let me eat it whole with you, pearl and all, and we will watch our happiness glow from inside my womb. We will let the juice flow over us, cover us, we will dance on the sand entwined like happy culebras, and we will laugh like we did before, until the tears drown us, laugh like we did before, until the tears drown us, laugh like we did before, together in the desert, drowning in the desert, making pearls, dreaming of pears, laugh like we. I knew, mi vida, I knew. I knew you. I knew...

you will take me with you now, no? I knew you would come back for me. Oh mi amor, mi vida, I am so tired, but I am ready. I have my pear, and I am ready. I know I am ready. I know I am. I know I. I know. I am. I know...

LOTERIA TABLA 4

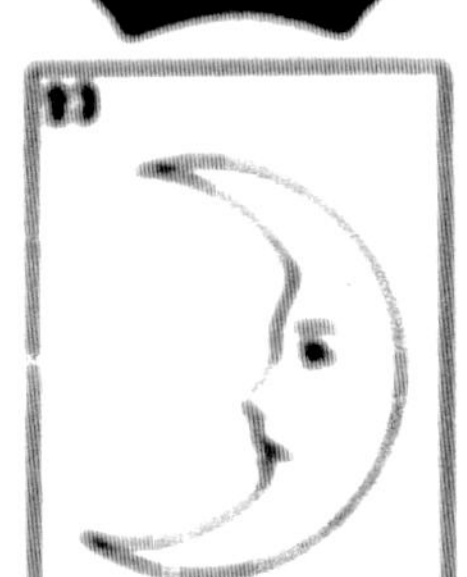

Uno dos y tres
el soldado pa'l cuartel.

9TH OF OCTOBER

He's flipping through the channels and he stops on a soccer game. One of the teams is called The 9th of October, and they are losing, and I wonder what that date is. The Americas are full of independence and revolutionary holidays. I laugh.

"What?"

"Nothing," I say, finishing my beer. A nice little buzz is setting in. "Let's go to the East Side."

"Sure," he says, and shrugs. Outside, orange streetlights paint the sidewalks and trees like some sick, bad dream. Staring out the window makes me feel like a zombie or something, like the orange darkness is trying to suck me into itself.

"Every time I come back to San Jose, I make a trip to the East Side," I say.

"It's good for the soul," he says, and I laugh at this also.

He puts on his jacket and grabs his keys. The jacket is brown leather. I put my A's cap on and grab another beer from the kitchen. We pull away from the curb in his car, and he puts a tape in. The wind feels good on my face and his Old Skool music leaks out the tiny speakers in metallic beats and squeaking synthesizers. Up Santa Clara Street, until it turns into Alum Rock. I see the Copa Cabana Club in a strip mall to my right and I remember playing video games at the arcade next door, waiting for my dad to come out drunk and tell me

I was addicted to them. I say, "Last I heard, my dad was working there."

"That's funny," he says. "Your dad's over there, and mine is right across the street." He points to the cemetery there, and I nod. His dad died in a car wreck when he was three. Up Alum Rock to White road, then right, then up East Side Road toward Joseph George Middle School as we let the music fill the silence.

"Do you remember the funeral?" I ask.

"Yeah. You know how I remember it?" I shake my head and watch Horace Cureton school pass by, with its dinosaur monkey bar structure standing in the shadows of the playground where I fought almost every day as a kid. "I remember standing over his grave, and when they lowered it, we were supposed to throw in a handful of dirt—you know, the family lays him to rest and shit. And...I remember, when my turn came, I reached down and tried to grab as much as I could in one hand...and thinking how I wanted to throw the most on the casket, I wanted to be the one to throw the most dirt, but my hand was too small. I remember feeling frustrated because I couldn't grab more dirt than that. I felt like it wasn't enough, like I could never hold enough in my hand. That's how I remember the funeral. That's how I know I didn't make up the memory afterward, you know?"

"Yeah, I know." We pull into the parking lot of Joseph George. I remember the day my mother told me she was going down to this school from our house to call a women's shelter. She was crying, mascara all streaked down her face and looking like a zombie, asking me if she could use my bike, and all I could do was just nod and imagine her riding down to the school on my bike to use the phone there. I remember she had trouble getting the bike off the porch, like it had too many strange parts and pieces sticking out all over the place and she couldn't get a good grip on it, and all I could do was just watch in silence through the front door screen and imagine her riding down the street to Joseph George all wobbly on the big Schwinn twelve speed, crying and wiping at the black streaks on her face.

He gets out of the car and I follow him on my side. We walk down past the pay phone and onto the campus. Concrete and asphalt cover everything now, but when we were here, it was mostly dirt with a few concrete walkways. There are no lights on this campus. It's dark and quiet and again I feel like a zombie, but now there is a certain stange comfort in this, and it feels good.

He picks up a rock and tosses it into a patch of bushes. "You know, every night after school, I would lay in bed and think back over the whole day, over everything that happened, every conversation and interaction with other people, and I would reconstruct it all, you know? Like, have the conversation over again, only this time, say what I should have said, and then make up the rest of the conversation from that point on. And I always felt so stupid for what I actually said, embarrassed, you know? My biggest wish was that I could turn back time and do it over again. Well, that was my second biggest wish."

"What was your first biggest wish?" I say.

"That I could stop time, you know? Mostly just so I could take girls' clothes off and look at them and shit." We laugh and I nod.

"Yeah, I know that one. Got a lot of good material out of it. It was like, the only way I could imagine I would ever get the chance to see a naked girl was if I had some kind of supernatural powers to alter reality. Otherwise, it just wasn't going to happen." The night wind is summer, soft, and warm. My eyes are adjusted now to the dark, and I can make out more clearly the shapes of benches and walls and windows.

"Do you wish you could turn it all back now and do it over again?" I say. He shakes his head.

"No, I'm pretty happy. And there's a lot of shit I wouldn't want to live through again. You?"

"Yeah, I do," I say. "In fact, I have a feeling I'll feel that way my whole life. I mean, I have this feeling no matter what I do, I'll always want to turn it back and do it over again right."

"So, you think you'll never do anything right?"

"Not right—I mean, I guess there's no real right way to do it. It's just that, I still stay awake at night and imagine how I would do it all over again, every night. I'm just never happy with how I do things, you know? No matter how good it turns out. I mean, I think things have turned out pretty okay for me, considering everything. But little things still bug me all the time. Like, when I graduated, and I gave my mom that certificate for helping me through college and all that, and everybody cried. Afterwards, I realized what I should have said.

Instead, I just read the certificate. I went over the speech I should have made, over and over at night trying to fall asleep, and it just killed me, because that moment...that moment will never be there again."

"But that was cool. I think what you did was great, man."

"But I missed an opportunity to say something really moving. I should have told the story of my first day of kindergarten, how I wanted to take the bus, and how she let me, and then followed the bus to my school in our orange truck so she could see me go in on my first day. I should have told that story, and then I could have said that that was how she helped me all these years to reach this goal, you know? Always letting me do my own thing, but at the same time, letting me know she was right there with me the whole time in case I needed her. It would have been perfect."

"But you would have regretted it though, right, because like you said, no matter what you say, you want to go back and change it later..."

"Yeah, that's the irony I guess."

"But then again, if you think about, that moment was just here right now again, when you told me about it." I nod. We are sitting now on a bench at the top of a hill that leads down to the basketball courts and the track. He is perched on the back of the bench like a bird. I lean back into the bench and breath the night air in. I imagine what we must look like to someone at a distance. Two more shadows melting into the bench and the chain-link fence and the leaves of the thin eucalyptus tree above us.

"I think maybe I'm really going to regret this, though." His voice is heavy, scratchy next.to me.

"What, the military?"

"Yeah. I mean, all I ever wanted to do was fly, and this seemed like the best way to do it. I just can't help feeling like maybe it's all bullshit, and I'm making a big mistake."

"Let me ask you something. Does it bother you that you might have to give your life for this country? I mean, really, is that cool with you?"

"Yeah, I figure somebody has to do it."

"But that's not really a reason. I mean, is this country, or any country really worth dying for?"

"Yeah, I think so. I know this is kind of gay, but somebody said once that the only thing worth living for and dying for is love. I love this country, so I guess yeah, I would die for it."

I am silent. A few cars pass on East Side Road, breathing into the silence with their soft mechanical whispers. I can hear the leaves of the tree above us moving gently. I watch him out of the corner of my eye. He takes a drink form his bottle of beer, then slumps forward slightly and stares at the ground.

"Look, it's not a question anymore of whether I'm willing to die or not. I'm leaving on a plane for Florida tomorrow at nine a.m., where I will train to be a navigator, and after training, I will be stationed somewhere where I will serve out my duty—about eight years—and then I will retire from the Air Force, maybe get a job with a commercial airline or something, or maybe give flying lessons or something."

"And if we go to war?"

"And if we go to war—which is highly unlikely, by the way, but—if we go to war, then I will serve my country as best I can."

"And die if need be."

"Well what do you want me to do? Like I said, there's no choice now. Now I just go along with it all." He takes another drink.

"You really love this country?" I say.

"Yeah, don't you?"

"Sort of, but I don't know about dying for it..."

"Well then what would you die for?" he asks. I stare down at the backboards and the nets swaying quietly from the hoops. I toss my empty bottle over the fence and listen as it hits the dirt hill with a soft thud and then rolls down to the asphalt of the basketball court. I think over his question and pull out a cigarette. I offer him one, but he doesn't smoke. I don't either, really.

"Did you know I played basketball for a year here, when I was in seventh grade?"

"Really? I never saw you play," he says.

"Well, I really sucked and they only put me in once in a while to give the real players a break. Coach Ventry only wanted me for my height–he had great plans for me as a Center the next year, and I think I broke his heart when I quit the team and started playing guitar. I hated that experience. That's one thing I would definitely not like to repeat. I think the only reason I did it was just to have something to do." We are silent for a few moments, and then he asks, again, "C'mon, what would you die for?"

"Well, certain people, I guess." I take a drag on the cigarette.

"Like who?"

"I don't know. Like my mom, or my family, or my girlfriend, I guess, or..."

"Or what?" The question hangs there above our heads and burns with a dull glow in the darkness. I flick some ashes, and they fall between my shoes like hot, gray snow.

"Or...that's it, I guess. People. Just people. You know, people I love."

It's quiet around us. I can feel the tree moving overhead, and I am grateful for the little swishing sound it makes. I do not look at him, but stare instead straight down at the basketball courts. The cigarette burns silently in my fingers, and I let the ash grow and then fall freely.

"Yeah, me too," he says quietly, and I nod. "You want to go get something to eat?"

"Yeah," I say. "Let's get out of here already."

El músico trompa de hule,
ya no me quiere tocar.

Rum Cake

There was a jazz musician living in the apartment next door to her. He was French. She was fascinated with his short dread locks and muscular arms and chest. He always wore a tight shirt and baggy blue jeans, with a cheap black blazer and heavy black steel-toed work shoes. He had a mustache and goatee, which he kept trimmed close to his face, and he wore a large gold loop earring through his left ear. They saw each other only in passing, as she left for work, or went out to get the mail. She knew he was French because of the name on his mailbox, and the way he said, "Hello." She knew he was a musician because she could hear him practicing on his saxophone and always saw him carrying his horn in its battered black case.

When she knew he was home, she would sometimes play her jazz records—Miles Davis, Ornette Coleman, Cal Tjader—anything to let him know she was hip. But he never came to her door, knocking, saying, "Hey, is that Coltrane?" She would start baking a rum cake, knowing she was out of sugar, and knowing this would therefore force her to go next door and borrow some from him. She knew that once they started talking, he would realize how much they had in common, would invite her in to chat, and would come over later on to have some rum cake and coffee with her. They would talk and laugh, she would excite him with her quick wit and musical knowledge, and he would make her shiver with his French accent, but she would never say, "Say something in French, Pierre....anything," because that was way unhip and childish for a cosmopolitan girl like her.

Of course, she could never get up the courage to ask for the sugar, even with the cold ingredients sitting there in a mess on her counter. She always ended up throwing away the beaten eggs and flour and cinnamon, eating the whole can of butterscotch frosting with a spoon, and washing it down with the bottle of rum. She would stand at the door, looking out the peephole at his door, her head pressed hard against the wood to keep her from falling down, and the bottle of rum hanging precariously from one hand.

Sometimes when he said "Hello," and smiled at her, she knew for certain he was interested in her. How could he smile like that and not be? The girls he brought home, always different, always beautiful, were just to make her jealous. She knew he wanted her, needed her. His smile said so.

But then she would go inside and look in the mirror, and step on the scale, and watch it rise to 130 pounds, 155 pounds, 280 pounds, 371 and a half pounds, up four from last week, and she would take off her clothes and step into the shower, let the warm water run down her face and body, and imagine he was there with her, naked, thin, beautiful next to her.

Me lo das
o me lo quitas.

Lotería

One of my Abuela's favorite stories to tell was The Birth of Vida and How She Got Her Name. I remember her descriptions of blood all over our kitchen table and blood all over our kitchen floor, and blood all over me, and screaming, and of my mother grabbing my Abuela's arm and digging her fingernails into her and crying out "Oh God, I'm dying mami! Mami, ayúdame-help me mami! Oh, ¡mi vida! Ay Dios, mi vida!" and of the steak knife they used to slice her open like a bloody melón. They could not pull me out. They had to slice her open around me before I suffocated, and it wasn't until after the funeral that they finally named me with her last words. It wasn't until two years after the funeral. My Abuela kept the knife in a box under my bed, uncleaned since it was used on my mother, and she would take it out and pass it around for everyone to gasp at when she told this story.

These details would wake me up every night and leave me sweaty and staring into the darkness of my hot room, and then the guilt of living by my mother's ultimate sacrifice, a detail which never failed to bring my Abuela to tears and which she reminded me of at least once a day every day of my life, would keep me awake the rest of the night until the sun came back and saved me again.

I'm too old now to be scared of stories like this; I know she was full of shit, but back then, I was just a little kid—and yet, sometimes, when I think of her, I still have to wipe pictures of a bloody melón from my mind, and this pinches me with the guilt I know I will never outgrow. And every month when the blood begins to flow, I imagine my mother Esperanza has come back to visit with me for a while and I make up conversations with her to ease the pain. I imagine I tell her everything. She strokes my long black hair with her fingers and holds my head in her young lap and I cry and tell her everything. I lay my head on her melon lap and cry and press up against its softness and cry and tell her everything from the beginning, and everything from before the beginning to now, and then after, and then forever, until I can't tell when is when, and she holds me and whispers, "It's alright, baby. I know. I'm here now, mi amor."

"Mami, why?"

"There's no reason, baby. Just because. Just because..."

"But I don't understand."

My Abuela sighs and crosses herself. "You ask too many questions mi 'ja. You're just like your mother, que Dios la cuide." She walks into the kitchen praying to her santos and shaking her head and trying to hide her tears. My black nine-year-old eyes follow her and then look down in guilt and I call after her.

"Abuela, I'm sorry. I won't ask any more questions."

"Come help me with these dishes." I drag a chair to the sink and then stand on it next to her.

"Look," she says, "God is mysterious and wonderful and He has a reason for everything He does. It's not our place to question Him, okay? Things just are the way they are. Some people He gave mamis, and some people papis, pero you have your Abuelo and me, and that's all you need. We love you, okay?"

"Okay."

We work in silence, my thin hands struggling to hold awkward blue plastic cups and immense brown plates which bend my wrists with their weight. I dry them with a rough orange towel. Abuela stands next to me, stout and comfortable, her short arms swirling soap around the dishes and rinsing them in deft movements I cannot keep up with. She is proud that she still has undyed black hair, and her cheeks still glow bright pink when she works or laughs. Abuelo's hair is all gray now, and she calls him her 'Gris Lightning.'

A jet plane passes over us and shakes the house on its way to San José International Airport. Her old wood cross rattles on its rusty nail next to the coo-coo clock that only works at 4:32 p.m.. Abuelo will be home soon. The falling sun lets us know we must hurry. I ask her again quietly to tell me how she met him, and as she wipes the last forks and knives clean, she sighs. Imagining along with her, I lean back against the pale yellow counter, standing on one foot and looking at her wide back, happy I have made her smile. She wipes her hands on her thighs and then slowly stirs a massive pot of soup.

"Well, your Abuelo came to California looking for gold pears with pearls in them," she begins, and immediately I see the pearls glowing bright in my mind and I see my Abuelo, mysteriously young like the black and white pictures on the living room window sill, wandering through shadowy black and white orchards in search of gold pears. "Only, he got lost in the train station in Lodi and there was nobody there who spoke Spanish. Except me. I saw him walking around like a huge lost puppy and I went up to him and tapped him on his big arm and he turned around and looked at me so sad. I said, 'Are you lost?' He was so embarrassed, but he was so happy to find somebody who spoke Spanish. He looked like he wanted to hug me and kiss me right there, he was so happy. I said, 'What's your name?' and he told me, and then I told him, 'Well my name is Dolores.' He told me he came from Nogales and he was looking for gold pears and I laughed and told him I didn't know where there was any such thing, but that he could probably work where we worked, so he said yes and came to live with us."

"How old were you, Abuela?" Anticipating her answer, my mind has already raced ahead to construct a shadowy picture of myself in the future, an eternity away: I am tall, so much taller, and I have long hair, and I am beautiful like the fuzzy pictures of Abuela in the living room.

"Fifteen."

"You're only fifteen?" He looked down at her in disbelief as they walked along an unpaved road toward her house, the train station fading behind them. "You look at least twenty-five."

Her cheeks blushed bright pink. "Well, how old are you?" A truck rattled next to them, sending up dust around them, and he laughed.

"I could almost be your daddy, little girl." She stumbled on a loose rock and almost fell into his massive side. He laughed again. "Watch out!" She pushed away from him roughly and walked on ahead of him faster, her face flushed in anger.

"Dolores, hey, what's wrong?" He caught up to her and passed her, then turned and walked backwards in front of her. "Did I say something bad?"

Her black eyes stared down at the road in silence. She tried to walk around him.

"Hey, look at me. I'm sorry. What did I do?"

She glanced up quickly and then back down. "You just-I just don't like-"

"What? What did I do?"

They stopped and stood facing each other. The sun cast its last rays onto the valley from behind the hills to the west. He looked so sad.

"I'm not a little girl, okay? Don't call me that."

He looked down into her smoky eyes and raised his eyebrows. "Really? Is that all?" He laughed loudly and she pushed around him again, angrier in his new laughter.

"Wait," he said as he ran around her to face her again and put his hands lightly on her shoulders. "I know you're not a little girl, Dolores. Of course I know that. You're a beautiful woman. Of course I can see that. I was just kidding, okay?"

His hands felt like comfortable mountains on her shoulders, and she reluctantly nodded her head yes. It was okay. "I was just making fun of myself, see? I'm already an old man.

I'm just laughing at myself because I could never have anyone so young and beautiful like you."

"Well, how old are you?"

"He was twenty-nine. He was such a gentleman. He came to live with us, and everybody loved him- my mami and papi, and my sisters, Nena and ChaCha, and my little brother Monchi, que Dios lo cuide." She crosses herself at the memory of The Soldier Brother Who Died in Korea, and I cross myself too for this man I have never known. "We got married a year later, and then your mama was born." She stops and stirs the pot quietly. She crosses herself again and I know she is crying, again, so I walk quietly outside into the velvet gold and purple sky.

The sun is a shrinking gold crescent, the bottom half of it already eaten by the earth's horizon. The Guadalupe River whispers across the street, and I walk to it from our blue house. There is an overpass bridge and I walk down a steep embankment to sit beneath the bridge on large, upheaved slabs of concrete which sprout and point their twisted, rusty claws of re-barre fingers at me. Here, the Guadalupe River is really a creek, no more than eight feet across, but we call it The River, and the thick trees and bushes around it The Jungle.

I feel cars rumble over the bridge on Hedding Street above me, and I listen for the sound of Abuelo's truck as I watch the green water move by. The water is dark green, almost black in the dying sunlight, and I sit and watch its mysterious movements. In the summer, we bring buckets and catch crawdads and frogs and put them inside and then poke at them with sticks to make them fight. When Manny lived across the street, we would walk along the rough banks of the creek all the way to Taylor Street. There is graffiti covering the concrete retaining walls underneath the bridge, black and red and white scrawls, unreadable signatures, and dirty words.

"Hey Vida, you know that word?" Manny points to a scribble on the slanted wall beneath the bridge. I am six. He is older. I pretend to know the word.

"Yeah, then what does it mean?" He is standing over me as I sit leaning back on my thin arms against a crumbling block of concrete. I push myself up and walk to the creek and leave him behind me.

"You know what it means, Manny. It's too nasty. I can't say it." I can feel my face hot and flushed and red. I search desperately for frogs. "There's some pollywogs."

"You don't know what it means. You're lying."

"Yes I do. I just can't say it."

"Why not? 'Cause you don't know, that's why. I'll tell you what it means. You wanna know?"

I am silent. He will tell me what it means. I crouch forward and let my long fingers disappear as they dangle halfway into the cool water. I imagine that when I lift them out again, the fingertips I cannot see beneath the surface of the murky water will be gone, erased by the magic of the moving water, or sucked away by hordes of hungry pollywogs.

"That's what people do to make babies."

The water moves over and around my fingers carefully. I study a rock jutting half-way out of the water, study its smooth angles and shades, examine the slick green and brown moss growing on the rock, then the grass which sprouts up around it and bends with the water, and then the movements of water skeeters that skim the surface as lightly and delicately as Father Martín's oily fingertip on my forehead when he blesses me with his crossing lines. The sun slices the creek into a million fine, sharp gold lines that dance on my eyes as the water moves between the steep green and brown embankments. The passing cars above us rumble into my ears. I can hear every displaced piece of gravel moved by the tires above us. I can hear every drop of water moving by. The sewer smell of the creek wraps around my head and I am dizzy.

"That's how people make babies, Vida. You know how they do that?"

My dizzy head shakes slowly and silently, and my eyes stare fiercely straight ahead into the water and the rock and the grass and the pollywogs. His voice is closer now behind me, and I realize that the voice is Manny. He has become the voice, and it is all that there is left of him. Just a voice floating behind me with no body.

"A guy and a girl get all naked under the covers in bed, and they kiss and stuff, and then his thing gets hard, and he gets on top of her and puts it inside her between her legs, and he moves up and down on her, and it feels real good, and he keeps on moving up and down until this milk stuff comes out of his thing inside her, and the girl has this egg inside her stomach and the milk stuff mixes with the egg, and that makes a baby inside her."

I am breathing hard now, scared, excited. I see my Abuelo on top of my Abuela moving straight up and down in harsh, vertical movements like some kind of manic human pogo stick, and his Thing is a forbidden shadow my mind does not dare imagine. Then I see Manny naked on top of a naked girl. The grass moves with the water. The rock is slick and mossy and dark, and the gray concrete lies around us in huge, stark blocks of smooth angles that deteriorate into jagged, broken edges.

"Have you ever seen a guy's thing?" Suddenly the voice is right beside me, right behind me, above me, inside me.

"No!" A frog splashes out at my face and I jump back and turn fast, and he is right there. I lose my balance bumping into him and fall back into the creek as he reaches out to catch me. I stand up quickly and run and claw my way up the embankment toward Regent Street, blindly digging my raw fingers into the loose mud and rocks and grass and broken concrete.

"Vida!" he calls after me. "Wait!"

I keep running, my hands are bleeding from scraping the rocks and concrete in the creek and on the hill, my clothes cling to me wet.

"I was just kidding," I hear him call out behind me, but I keep running to my blue house.

"Vida!"

I run across Regent Street to the house. My Abuela is standing on the white porch in her worn apron, calling me. I expect to find Abuelo home. I expect to see his rusting, yellow 1962 Chevrolet Apache utility truck sitting at an angle halfway across our gravel driveway and the rough brown grass of our dead lawn, an unpainted wrought iron screen door tied to the iron railing of the truck bed with a frayed yellow rope. "I'm coming!" I yell out. The sun has finally disappeared completely, and as I run across the street, the deep violet light is quietly melting into blackness with the memory of Manny and the frog.

"Where's Abuelo?" I ask, running up onto the porch out of breath.

"Oh, he's going to be late again tonight mi 'ja. Come inside and eat and then maybe we'll play Lotería before you go to bed."

"Can I watch T. V.?"

"We'll see. Go wash your hands."

After dinner, Abuela takes out the yellow Lotería box. She hands me some dry beans to use as markers, then shuffles the cards. The T. V. sits quiet in the corner of the living room. I spread my beans out in even lines on the green carpet of the living room floor and lay flat on my stomach and Abuela sits back against the worn couch.

"Okay, ready?" She holds the cards face down in her hand. I nod yes.

"The first card is..." she pauses, then flips it over. "El Melón. The melon. 'Me lo das o me lo quitas.'" Abuela knows all the poemas that go with each card by heart. I have El Melón on my card, and I place a bean on its picture.

"Next is...La Bota. The boot. 'Una bota igual que l'otra.'" I recite the poema with her because it is one of my favorites, but I don't have La Bota on my card. She does. "Next: La Pera. The pear. 'El que espera, desespera.'" I have La Pera, and place a bean carefully in the center of the pear. Another jet passes over the house and rattles the window.

"Where's Abuelo?" It is late.

"Oh, he had some business to take care of." Abuela tries to smile, but I can see the tightness around her mouth, and she has been pale since before dinner. "Next card...El árbol. The tree. 'El que a buen árbol se arrima, buena sombra le cobrija.' Next is El Catrín. The gentleman. 'Don Ferruco en la Alameda su bastón quería tirar.'" I have the gentleman, right next to La Pera.

"Let me do the next one." I am trying to cheer her up, to make her laugh again and smile.

"Sure, but you have to say the poema," she says absently as she hands me the cards. She takes a sip from the small glass in her hand, then sets it down and lets the ice clink together loudly. I can smell the whiskey in the glass and on her breath.

"Okay, the next card is..." I pause extra long to get her attention, grinning as I pull the card slowly and flip it over. "El Soldado! The soldier." I do not know the poema for this card, so I have to look at the list and read it. "'Uno dos y tres, el soldado pa'l cuartel.'" I have El Soldado and put a bean there, then look at Abuela's card. She has El Soldado too, but she hasn't put a bean there yet.

"Hey, you have it too Abuela." I point to it, then look up at her and see that she's looking out into the darkness of our driveway through the blurred reflection of the window, sighing, her eyes watering.

"Monchi was so cute. Ramón. We called him Ramonsito, and he always hated it. My papi called him Gallo Cachetón because his face was so chubby. He was always joking around, always making everybody laugh. I remember when he finally left for Korea."

I am silent. I see Tío Monchi. I see my Abuela crying.

"Don't cry."

"But my baby's leaving. Ay, me muero!" his mother wailed as she buried her face into his father's chest and pounded on him with her tiny balled fists, her body wracked by her sobs. Dolores leaned into her husband and cried silently. He held her around her shoulder. The dust of the train station hung in the air around them all.

"I'll be back, mami. I promise. Don't worry. I probably won't even be fighting. They'll need somebody to cook the beans." He paused. "Papi, take care of her."

"I will. Pórtate bien, okay? Sea hombre." His father walked forward and tried to smile. "Gallo Cachetón," he said as he embraced his son roughly. He pulled away and turned around to hide his tears. His mother stepped forward and clung to his neck, wailing his name over and over, her tears soaking his uniform. His father had to pull her away as the porter gave second call for boarding.

"Be careful, Ramón," Dolores whispered to him as she hugged him and kissed his cheek. "You'll always be my little brother. Please write to us."

"I will."

Her husband stepped forward and took his hand firmly in one of his own massive hands. "Ten cuidado," was all he could say, and Ramón nodded silently. Esperanza clung to her father's other hand. Ramón stooped down and pulled her to him.

"Bye mi 'ja. Take care of your mami and papi."

"Goodbye Tío Monchi. I love you." She pressed her face into him and stretched her arms around his chest. His uniform was rough on her face. The twins stood quietly behind their parents, and Ramón stood up and hugged them both together, one arm for each sister.

"Be good girls," he said. They nodded and cried and pressed together between their brother's palms and he kissed each on the cheek. The porter called final boarding, and as Ramón leaned down to pick up his new green duffel bag, his mother ran forward again and pressed a hot brown bag into his hands.

"Por si te da hambre," she said, grasping his hand tightly, desperately, as she handed him the tamales she had stayed up cooking the night before. "Goodbye mi 'jo. Que Dios te vendiga." She still held onto him as he stepped up into the train and put the bag and the tamales at his feet. The train began to move, and still she held onto his hand. He felt the tears coming, but now they were all too far back to see him, and he let them fall. Only his mother saw, and that was okay. She ran until she couldn't keep up with the train, then let go with one final wail. He watched her disappear slowly, bent over in the brown dust, crying out to him. He saw his father and his sisters and his brother-in-law and his niece run to her and help her up and hold her as she cried and cried, watching her only son fade into the haze of the San Joaquín Valley. "My baby was crying," was all she could say.

"He was crying."

I watch silently as Abuela sobs and crosses herself. I cross myself too, again. "I'm sorry mi 'ja. What's the next card?" She smiles through her tears and blows her red nose, then takes another drink, and I hold my breath as I flip the next card over. It is the frog.

"La Rana. The frog. 'Al ver a la verde rana, que brinco pegó tu hermana.'" I have the frog and place a bean next to his mouth. "Look Abuela, he's eating the bean."

She laughs as she wipes at her wet face. "Yes, he's eating it."

"The next one is...El Apache. I don't know the poema. You say it Abuela."

"Okay, pero only this one. You're supposed to do it. '¡Ay Chihuahua! cuánto apache con pantalón y huarache.' I giggle and place a bean on the picture of El Apache.

"Here, you do the cards now." I hand her the cards. "I don't know the poemas good enough. You do it better."

"Okay pues. The next card is...El Borracho. The drunk guy. '¡Ah! que borracho tan necio, ya no lo puedo aguantar.'" El Borracho is above La Rana on my card, and once again, I begin to get the feeling that Abuela has shuffled the cards according to my card so that I will win.

"Abuela, did you fix it so I would win?"

"What? No way Jose," she says, and I giggle. As if to prove it to me, she draws next Las Jaras, the arrows. "See, you don't have Las Jaras, do you? But I do." She places a bean on the arrows.

"My name is Vida, not Jose," I say, laughing.

"Vida, Jose, what difference does it make?"

"You're silly. What's the next card?"

"La Luna. The moon. 'El farol de enamorados.'" I have La Luna, and my suspicions return, but I am too busy picturing two lovers walking under the light of the moon.

"And the next card is...La Sirena. The mermaid. 'Con los cantos de sirena no te vayas a marear.'" I have this card too. She stares at the card in her hand, and I know already what she is thinking.

"Tell me about her, please. What was she like?" I know it will make her cry, but I can never pass up a chance to hear about her-not about the birth, or the steak knife, or her bloody sacrifice, or any of those things that make me cry and give me nightmares, but about her. Just her.

"She was beautiful, like La Sirena, with long honey brown hair. But such a spirit. She always had to get her way. Always arguing with your Abuelo and me."

"Is that why she left?"

My Abuela is silent, looking down at the card. She is pale, and her mouth is tight at the corners. Her lips are tight and pale pink, almost white. "Yes. That's why she left. She was only fifteen years old when she ran away. She just left, and then five months later we got a postcard from Los Angeles.

Palmas. A setting sun. And then nothing, for five years. Five years I worried and prayed and lost hope. I thought she was dead. I thought so many horrible things, ay Dios Mío, things you can't even imagine yet. And then one day she just showed up at the front door."

I look at our front door and imagine her standing there, her long hair flowing behind her like La Sirena in the picture. She is holding a suitcase in one long hand, standing silently behind the screen door.

"Mi 'ja," she whispered through the screen as she held one hand to her mouth.

"Hi Mami," Esperanza whispered back, setting the suitcase down and smiling cautiously at her mother.

"It's a miracle!" Dolores shouted as she pushed open the creaking screen door into the heat of August and threw her arms around her daughter.

"I missed you so much mami," Esperanza cried as they held onto each other.

"Oh me too, me too. I was so worried. What happened? I thought so many bad things. What happened to you? Oh come inside. Oh mi 'ja, you're so beautiful, so grown up. Here, give me your suitcase."

Esperanza laughed. "No mami, I can get it. It's too heavy for you." They came inside out of the heat and sat close to each other on the couch in front of a whirring metal fan.

"How did you get here?"

"I took a taxi from the Greyhound station."

"Oh. Are you thirsty? Here, let me make you something

to eat. You hungry? You want some ice tea?"

"Yes mami. I could use something to drink. Maybe a beer."

"A beer? Pero mi 'ja, you can't-"

"Mami, I'm twenty." Dolores stared at her, unbelieving, then walked silently into the kitchen to get a beer.

When she returned, Esperanza was sitting back comfortably in the fan's breeze, the top buttons of her dress undone, her shoulders and neck and upper chest exposed, and her long hair pulled and bunched up behind her head as she leaned back against the couch. "Thank you Mami," she said as she took the beer and rubbed her neck and chest with the cold bottle. "Here. You might need a drink."

"Oh no, you know I don't drink."

"I have something to tell you."

"What is it, mi 'ja?" Outside, a lawnmower droned in the heat.

"Mami, I'm pregnant."

Silence.

"Did she look like me?" I ask again. Abuela is still silent. I stare at the card in her hand, waiting as she rocks back and forth. Finally she nods and sighs.

"Yes. She looked so much like you, but not so tall." A car passes outside and my heart jumps because I think it is Abuelo, but the car keeps moving down Regent Street.

"Did she sleep in my room?"

Silence.

"Did you hear me?"

"Yes."

"And? What is it? I know. You're too embarrassed to talk about it, aren't you? Jesus, mami, I'm a grown up here. Look how old you were when you had me. I'm pregnant. I have sex, and I'm pregnant, and now I really need your help." She was leaning forward now with the bottle of beer hanging from one hand between her legs, her other hand resting on her mother's knee. Her eyes searched Dolores' pale face.

"Who's the father?"

The fan whirred quietly. A dog barked across the street against the ever-present sound of the lawnmower. "I'm not sure."

"Ay Dios Mío!" Dolores stood and crossed herself and walked rapidly to the kitchen. Esperanza watched her go, then listened to the clanging dishes as her mother scrubbed plates and bowls and cups she had already washed twice that day. She fell back into the couch again and finished the beer, then took off her tired sandals, stretching her long, thin toes in the fan's wind before she stood and walked quietly to the kitchen. Dolores worked furiously at the sink. Esperanza leaned barefoot against the frame of the kitchen door and watched her mother's thick back and stout arms. The water hissed from the faucet as it sprayed onto pots and pans.

"Mami, I know sex is something we don't talk about in this house, but I can't run away and let you off that easy again. This time I really need your help."

Dolores turned suddenly and faced her daughter. "You're a disgrace! Desgracia! What do you think your father will say when he hears this? What do you think he'll say?"

"To hell with what he says! I don't care!" The water spit into the sink behind Dolores. "I don't care. He's the reason I left here in the first place. You know that. I know you do. Don't stand there and tell me you don't know. Don't stand there and pretend everything here was so wonderful. You know why I left. You helped make me go."

"You're crazy. You were always crazy, and disrespectful, and now you come into my house acting like a puta, drinking beer and cursing just because you think you're a grown-up now. You don't even know who the father of your child is!" She was wringing a towel with her shaking hands and leaning against the kitchen counter. Her face was bright red and tight. "You're worse than a puta! At least a puta does it to survive."

"You don't know all the things I did to survive! You don't know..." Esperanza's voice broke and trailed off elliptically. They stood silent, staring at nothing.

"Look," Esperanza began again, her red eyes down in defeat. "I'm sorry. I won't be disrespectful anymore. I just need your help badly. I need you to help me, okay? I don't have anywhere else to go." She was crying now, and she walked toward her mother, barefoot, her arms outstretched. "Forgive me mami. Please. I don't have anywhere to go. You're all I have. Forgive me."

"Not until you go to Father Martín and confess all your sins and take communion with me."

"Okay, okay. I'll go. Right now. Right now, if you want. Just say you'll help me. Please. Just say it and then I'll know everything will be okay." The water continued pouring into the sink. Dolores looked down at the towel in her hands.

"Okay, I'll help you." Reluctantly, she placed her arms around her daughter's thin shoulders and held her as she cried into her.

"I'm sorry mami. Do you still love me, mami?"

"Yes, she slept in your room."

I am silent. I count the spaces left on my card. La Muerte, El Diablito, La Mano, El Alacrán, La Palma, La Estrella, El Mundo.

"We don't have to play anymore, Abuela. I'm tired anyway." I fake a yawn and stretch my arms out. Where is Abuelo?

"Oh mi 'ja, I'm sorry. I just get so sad thinking about how life turns out. Everybody gets a card, all different. Some people El Catrín, some people get El Borracho, some people get La Estrella or El Diablito. Everybody different mi 'ja, and we just have to accept it because that's what we get. That's the card Dios gave us. But one thing is always the same."

I feel the tears coming and want so bad to jump up and run to my bed. Abuela holds up a card.

"Everybody has La Muerte, mi 'ja. We all die. Everybody has La Muerte on their card." La Muerte is a grinning skeleton who holds a strange spear. I see that she is right. I have La Muerte on my card, and so does she.

"Sooner or later, Vida, La Muerte comes up. And that's why I'm so sad. For Monchi and your mama it was too much sooner." She is crying, holding the card to her chest. I push myself up and walk to the darkness of my bedroom, closing my door quietly behind me to block out the sounds of her sobs. My curtain is open, and the moon shines brightly into my room. I change into pajamas and climb into bed, knowing Abuela will not bother me to brush my teeth tonight.

I bring the covers up to my chin and stare out the window at the moon, wondering where Abuelo is and when he will come home. I think about La Muerte grinning at me, waiting for me, and I close my eyes out of fear. Even with my eyes closed, though, I still see him coming for me like he came for my mother and Tío Monchi. I open my eyes again to look at the moon's welcome light, but soon my eyes grow heavy and I fall into dreams.

La Muerte is holding up a card behind me with his picture on it, and my hand reaches out in slow motion with a bean that grows heavier and heavier, so heavy I can no longer carry it with just one hand. My card stretches out of sight at my feet, and the bean is now a huge mottled brown and white melon I carry from picture to picture looking for La Muerte, and searching for my mother, and wondering when he will come home and kiss me goodnight. I am crying out loud, Oh God, where are you, where are you, and I cannot breath, and my lungs push hard against the inside of my chest and I am going to explode, and then suddenly...then suddenly...I am standing on El Diablito, and he rises up next to me out of the card with his red spear and red pointy tail and his evil smile and goatee and horns.

"Relax, Vida, it's okay." El Diablito caresses my hot forehead and the card disappears and I am lying down in my bed again. El Diablito stands over me and caresses my head, pushing back my long hair with one red hand. The weight of the bean rests softly now on my stomach, and I finally breathe as he whispers to me. I feel his hand moving all over my face and neck, and then all over my body, and it is soft and cool. It feels good.

Suddenly my eyes open wide into the darkness of the room. The moon is now a fading sliver that peaks in through my window and sends a sharp blade across Abuelo's eyes as he sits next to me on the edge of my bed, looking over me. I can hear him breathing.

"Good morning, mi 'ja. You were having a bad dream." I cannot see his mouth as it speaks to me, but I can tell it is smiling. He does not move. His massive hand does not move, but I can feel it. The room is shadowy and dark, and the moonlight lets me see only his red eyes and his sagging cheeks and the dull silver of his hair. I am frozen. The sound of Abuela's snoring down the hall is sharp in my ears.

"It's not morning," I whisper.

"I know. I'm just kidding. You're so beautiful mi 'ja. Such a pretty young lady." He strokes away a strand of my hair with one huge finger. "Remember when you were little and you were playing with the scorpion in México, and the other kids didn't tell you what it was, y casi te picó? Now you're almost all grown up." I can smell his breath.

My head barely nods. The hand does not move. The smoke and grease and steel smell of his sweat-stained clothes grips me, and his breath makes me dizzy. My eyes stare at the wall as he talks to me, stare at the cracks that line the wall like thin, intricate spider webs, and I listen to my Abuela snoring, and the frogs and crickets outside my window. Mami, I call out in silence.

"You'll be a woman soon, y entonces? You'll leave your poor abuelos all alone, no? I'll be so sad. I'll miss you. Will you miss your poor Abuelo? Will you miss me?" He bends down to kiss my face and I hold my breath as his cold, wet lips slide across my cheek and down to my neck like thick worms. His nostrils blow hot air at my skin. His hand moves slightly, roughly, and I feel his lips pressing behind my ear. "Oh Vida, you're so beautiful, just like your mama," he whispers, and I cannot move. I see the shape of his head as he kisses my neck, I see his immense hulking back as he leans into me, and I wonder what card this is. I wonder why my card has this picture on it. Why? Why Mami? I think to myself as I feel the tears come, as I feel his nose rub against my neck, as I feel his hot breath on me. As I feel his hand on me.

Suddenly his enormous hand pulls away and he stands up quickly and clumsily as the light turns on in the hall. I see his gray chest hair poking out of the unbuttoned, wrinkled blue work shirt he wears every day. He almost falls back, one finger pressed to the spittle that glistens on his mischievously grinning lips.

"Dolores," he calls out.

"Is that you?" Her sleepy voice comes before her shadow crosses my doorway, and then she is standing there.

"Hi mi amor. I was just telling Vida goodnight." His voice is slurred as he stumbles toward her. Abuela's eyes are wide open now and they stare at me as I lay under my covers, under the blankets she made for my mother.

"Where have you been?" Her voice is no longer sleepy, but sharp, as she looks from me to Abuelo and back again.

"Oh, here and there, and everywhere." His massive arms flail in clumsy nonchalance. "I'm a busy man, you know that. A busy-ness man. Hah! I have to do my busy-ness and take care of mi FA-MIL-IA." He says this last word too loud, almost yelling it. His arms are now wrapped heavily around her and she tries to push him away, but it is no use. He is too big. "Now I'm ready to see my sexy honey," he mumbles into her neck as his wet lips and tongue press against her. He rocks and leans into her with his hips.

"Go to bed and wait for me there, okay? I'll be there." Abuela is staring only at me now, and I avoid her black eyes by looking down at the carpet.

He is suddenly quiet and motionless as he leans against her. He pulls away. "Oh yeah, I'll be waiting for you." He grins and winks at me. "But first, I think I'm going to be sick." With his last words, vomit explodes out of his mouth through the open doorway in a line that stretches across the carpet and walls from my room to the hall, and he stumbles to the bathroom. I hear his gagging as Abuela comes and sits next to me.

"Remember mi 'ja, some things just happen and there's nothing we can do," she whispers. "That's just the way Dios meant for it to be, okay? Your Abuelo is a good man. He takes care of us and feeds us and pays the bills, but nobody is perfect."

I know she knows, I can see that she knows, and my head nods in silence. She stands, pale, her face tight, and goes to the bathroom, closing my door behind her as she leaves. The stench of his vomit grows inside my room. It overwhelms me and I feel my throat gag. I can hear Abuela washing him off in the bathroom, struggling to get him out of his clothes as the water runs loudly first in the sink and then in the shower.

"I love you Dolores." His voice echoes harshly on the bathroom walls through his sobs.

They are just sounds now. Echoes of voices and movements in some other world have replaced my Abuelo and Abuela. They are just sounds.

The tears fall as I follow the sounds into the bedroom. She is a voice that says, "No, let's wait baby," and then he is a shout, then a slap, and then, they are silence. The bed begins to creak and he is a grunting, and she is a moan "No, no," that repeats over and over again. "Shut Up!" and then she is a silence—she is nothing.

The bed bangs and creaks, and suddenly Manny slithers into and out of my head again like some silent black and white whisper. The sound is Abuelo on top, moving up and down roughly, sharply, in and out...*that's how people make babies, Vida...you know how they do that...all naked under the covers in bed, and they kiss and stuff...his thing gets hard...his thing...and he gets on top of her and puts it inside her between her legs...his thing...shhhh....and he moves up and down on her, and it feels real good...doesn't that feel good, mi 'ja...doesn't that feel good vida...and he moves up and down on her...up and down on her...up and down on her and...Shut Up!...and...down...and...up...and...why...and...down...and...upanddown andupanddownandupanddownand..*.over, and suddenly my mind is just another sound, just another silent voice, which cries out, 'Why? Why? Mami, why?'

And now, I imagine Esperanza holds my head in her soft lap, and I press up against her melon belly as I find myself, just as she did some twenty years ago, on a bus bound for Los Angeles where Tía Nena and her family wait for us. They know only that someone has made me pregnant, but they do not know who. My hand rests on my round, melon belly. I stare out the dark tinted brown glass at the yellow and brown land melting in silent waves next to the bus, and I can feel her pushing up against the inside of my belly. I can feel her crying and calling out to me. I can feel her asking me. I can feel her pressing up against my belly from inside and calling to me.

I stroke my soft belly, and I cry and tell her everything. I feel her pressing up against my softness and I cry and tell her everything from the beginning, and everything from before the beginning to now, and then after, and then forever, until I can't tell when is when, and I hold her inside and whisper, "It's alright, baby. I know. I'm here now, mi amor."

"Mami, why?"

"There's no reason, baby. Just because. Just because..."

"But I don't understand."

"Just because..."

...and then Los Angeles. I see her life, her story, play itself out in that strange city. I see a girl with black hair and bright, shining black eyes that stare through me with the honesty and the void of a soul which no longer exists—no: a soul which never had the misfortune of existing in the first place, because that is one myth I promise I will never try to fool you into believing. I see you at four, and five, and six, my baby, my own baby for me to love, my own hija, with your own stories to tell, and I see myself telling you the stories of your own life, stories I will try more than anything to give happy endings to, regardless of their beginnings. I wonder: how to begin? I think I will say, "You were born in Los Angeles in the year 1980, when I was fourteen years old." Maybe. Or maybe I'll just say, "How to begin?" Later, I'll tell you the real beginning before the beginning before the beginning and so on, and so on. I will tell you the story of your mother and your grandmother, and your great-grandmother, and of golden pears, and of bloody melones, and of frogs, and soldiers, and diablitos—but only when you're ready to understand. Until that time, I will try to protect you and give you only good stories to remember. I promise to hold you in my lap and try to give you strength, and some way of continuing on, in spite of everything.

I don't understand either, mi 'ja. Maybe there is no truth, no explanation to give. All I know is that there is pain, and hope, and life, and then nothing. Nothing but these stories, and maybe not even that. Only these stories I tell myself over and over again to make some sense of it all, or maybe, to make no sense at all; only these stories I will tell you over and over again to try to help you make sense...sense...make sense...all I can do is hold you in my belly and in my lap and in my arms, and tell you these stories and...and...I'm so tired...and...all I can do, all I can do, mi amor...in the end, all I can do is...is give you these stories...these stories...and offer you the comfort that you are not alone, the comfort that you are not...

"Ma," I say. She's got a line of spit that drags from her bottom lip to her chest. The sides of her mouth are all crusty as she moves it around silent words. There's an empty bottle of bourbon lying on its side next to her feet in their pale blue slippers. Her hair is frizzed out and matted, graying here and there, and I can see her sad, sagging breasts with their dull stretch mark lines under the threadbare robe I gave her four Christmases ago. I close the robe and shake her shoulder.

"Ma," I say again. She mumbles something incoherent, I can hold you in my belly, I'm so tired, something like that, and I know she's telling her stories to herself again. "Ma, why don't you go to bed?" I lay my hand on top of hers and shake it gently. Her hand is dry and wrinkled, cold under my warm palm. Outside, the rain falls steadily. I can hear it beating up against the window. A car passes, splashing through a puddle where the street dips. The clock strikes a muted two a.m. The T.V. emits a dull gray noise, and its chaotic lights make dancing shadows on her face.

"Come on Ma, let's go." I jingle my keys next to her ear, softly, and she opens her eyes. They are bleary and orange in the streetlight seeping in through the open curtains.

"Mi 'ja, where have you been? I've been waiting for you. It's so late." Her voice is thick with the bourbon. She raises a hand and pats at her hair, aimlessly, as if she is trying to straighten and fix it, but more out of habit than anything else. She looks around her in confusion. She's not sure where she is. "I have some stories to tell you, mi 'ja. You know how I got my name? Let me tell you the story of The Birth of Vida and—"

"Not tonight Ma. It's late. Maybe later, okay? Right now you should get to bed. It's cold. Come on." I take her arm and lift her out of the chair. She's heavy, and she almost falls back, but I hold onto her thick arm tightly with both hands. I drape her arm over my shoulder and start walking her down the hall to her room. We stumble into the walls a few times. The smell of the bourbon is strong, but not strong enough to cover up the smell of her body. She hasn't bathed in a week.

"Get my pills, mi 'ja, I need my pills..."

"Okay, just lay down," I say. I set her down on the mattress. It has a deep indentation in the middle, and stains all over. There are no sheets. She curls into a fetal position, and I look around for some blankets and a pillow. I cover her with a thin quilt her grandmother made. She is already asleep again, but she's talking, telling her stories to herself, and I sit down next to her and put my hand on her head. Every once in a while, a clear word or two will work its way out, but then, just as quickly, her voice sinks back into muddy incoherence. I stroke her rough hair back with my fingers and watch the lines of rain fall with their soft rhythm outside her window.

La muerte

siriqui siaca.

ENTREPRENEUR

I was a traveling life insurance salesman. I had an old, dusty blue Plymouth with oversized tailfins and chrome everywhere. The tires were enormous and white-walled, the interior was broken-in gray leather. Insurance forms, brochures and policies, and maps were scattered in a mess on the back seat. I made money selling the policies to poor farmers. I would stop at small bars and taverns along rural highways during happy hour, get some food and drinks, and then start explaining to these poor, illiterate and uneducated laborers and farmers the necessities of life insurance.

At first, they didn't pay much attention to me. But then I began explaining my policies to them in an entertaining fashion, throwing in bawdy jokes and raunchy anecdotes. I would read palms, pointing out imaginary lines and marks which promised a beautiful wife, strong healthy children, a great sex life. But invariably, the life line would somehow always be cut short by some sudden, terrible mishap with farming machinery or some mysterious unnamed illness. They seemed to find this very entertaining, so I even took up juggling, which I used to illustrate the precarious balance of life and death. Soon, I had a polished Vaudeville-style routine which I took from town to town and which earned me just enough to get by. I wore a red and white striped suit with a vest and a bowler hat, and one of those trick squirting flowers on my lapel. And when I opened my briefcase of forms and policies, a bright bouquet of fake flowers would pop out.

The act seemed to work okay for a while. But then it wasn't enough, because I had become more of a clown, a comedian, and it became more and more clear that I wasn't being taken seriously. So I stopped wearing the large yellow squirting flower, toned down my jokes, spent less time reading palms. But I was still too polished for my own good, and people began looking forward to my visits as if I were the circus coming to town. They would set up makeshift stages, and whole families would come out to see me during the day. Mothers would bring smudge-faced kids with lollipops, and the kids would scream in laughter and delight, and at night, I would put on a more raunchy show for their husbands and fathers in the bars.

They loved the show, but no one wanted to buy insurance. I became more and more desperate, because the little change and tips I received for my performances were just not enough. Finally, I decided I would have to take drastic measures to convince these people that they needed to buy my life insurance policies. My plan was to target a prominent member of the community, preferably someone with a large family. I would then kill him and make his death look like a horrible accident. Then, after about a week, I would drive back into town while everyone was still talking about the misfortunes of the family of the deceased. I would begin my routine, praising the dead man if he had purchased a life insurance policy, dabbing at my eyes with a white handkerchief and shaking my head in disbelief if he hadn't.

My plan worked. People were frightened and moved so much they would buy several policies. If they didn't, other members of the community would look at them with scorn and deride them with questions like, "Don't you care 'bout your family, Billie? You want your kids to end up like Jones', hungry and poor and waitin' in the welfare line? You want your wife to get desperate for money like Lisa Mae, God save her poor wretch'd soul?" I hardly had to do any selling at all.

Within two months, I had broken all sales records and become Regional Sales Leader. After four months, I was top seller for the whole Tri-State area, then the Western Division, and finally, for the whole country. I was promoted to National Division Manager, made a member of the Board of Directors, and eventually, CEO, all within a few years. My record was unbeatable, and my teams of salesmen exhibited the same talent for sales as I had, because I trained them in my foolproof secret system.

I grew so wealthy I was able to buy out the other shareholders and become the primary stockholder of the company's vast assets. Soon, I had a large, sprawling homestead in the country, a high-rise penthouse in the city, vacation homes on several tropical and Mediterranean islands, two or three yachts, a private jet, a fleet of luxury automobiles, a professional women's softball team, two frozen yogurt franchises, a bubble gum factory, several small Southeast Asian Pacific island nations, and a museum filled with instruments of death from throughout the ages. There were sickles, knives, guns, iron maidens, spears, poisoned arrowheads, an atomic bomb, and vials filled with some of the deadliest viruses and diseases ever created by man.

I lived in unbelievable luxury, with an army of servants at my beck and call twenty-four hours a day. My every need and desire was met. I ate ten to twenty meals every day, prepared by the finest chefs in the world. I staged massive orgies with hundreds of people which lasted weeks. I was one of the richest men in the world.

But, eventually, it wasn't enough, because I had become obsessed with death. I began searching for a way to avoid it. I hired the brightest and most successful Nobel Prize-winning scientists and doctors from around the world. I avoided any activity which might be even remotely strenuous, then ceased all activity completely. I would lie in bed all day and night, deep underground in a special chamber constructed to keep out all sunlight, radiation, air borne chemicals and micro-organisms, and non-purified oxygen, while my team of scientists devised new bitter-tasting drugs and formulas to help me live forever. I took them all, firing the scientist if the drug made me ill, paying him extra if the drug made me feel good. Soon, I was being pumped full of opium and other pleasure-inducing drugs, because the scientists just wanted me to feel good and pay them more. After a few months of this, I had become a hollow-eyed, burned out addict. I fired my whole team of scientists and admitted myself into a detoxification center for treatment.

At the center, I came to realize that my quest for eternal life could never be successful in the material world. No, I knew that if I wanted to live forever, I would have to pursue the spiritual. My treatment program was the quickest in the history of the center. Doctors were amazed at my ability to quit cold turkey and successfully complete the 3 month program in only a few days. I became a model for other addicts. They made posters and television commercials with me, and the ad campaign was so successful, they had to build another center to handle the large number of addicts who came pouring in every day. They offered to pay me large sums of money to run the clinic, but I was tired of money, and wanted to pursue my spiritual quest.

So I renounced all worldly goods and set out on foot through the Himalayas. I carried with me only a small knapsack for food. I wore sandals and simple brown trousers, and a white shirt I had sewn myself. After weeks of wandering through the mountains, I came upon a Buddhist monastery. The monks took me in, and I began to study their faith.

Within days, I was achieving states of meditative perfection which other monks had taken years, even decades to reach. I became a spiritual leader, an example of piety and righteousness, a model for others to follow. I used my experiences in the world of material excess to explore spiritual issues. I was loved by everyone in the monastery. Soon, people began to come from hundreds, thousands of miles away to seek my advice.

I became the leader of the monastery, and once again, my name was famous around the world. So many people began making the journey up the tortuous mountains that we decided to build a modest five-story inn where they could stay, along with a small nuclear-powered generator for electricity. To finance the construction, we incorporated the monastery and held a successful initial public offer of stock in the corporation. We also had to charge visitors a nominal fee, but of course, they were more than willing to pay for a few minutes with me. I would listen to their life stories, read their palms, and then give them advice on how they should live.

Soon, we had to add another two stories onto the inn. Some of the monks began complaining that working at the front desk, cleaning rooms, taking reservations, and serving meals was all taking too much time out of their meditation schedules. So to address their concerns, we hired a full time staff of clerks, bell hops, a concierge, chefs, a sales and catering staff, and a security force of trained baboons.

And there was so much foot traffic on the small, winding road leading up to the monastery that environmentalist groups soon began expressing concern about the impact on the plant and animal life. We agreed that this could be a problem, so we constructed a small airfield and bought several Cessna planes to fly visitors in and out. This worked for a few months, but as our popularity grew even more, we found that we had to expand the airfield to five runways, and traded in the Cessnas for a couple of Learjets.

The inn grew so popular we decided to add a golf course, several heated, in-door Olympic-sized swimming pools, Jacuzzis, a gym, a business work center with facsimile machines, personal computers and modems, and video teleconferencing equipment, along with a large gift shop where we sold T-shirts, coffee mugs, Frisbees, giant over-sized bendable pencils, calendars, stationery, personal computer mouse pads, and post cards, all imprinted with my likeness and name, along with a five to ten-word quote of wisdom. At first, I actually wrote the quotes, but then I found myself too busy and had to hire a full-time in-house staff which I called my "Wisdom Writers." They wrote things like, "Live for today, tomorrow" and "Eternal life is shorter than you think."

We decided to set up a second monastery in Barbados so that the monks and I could spend some quality time in a more pleasant climate. We constructed a world-class five star resort on the beach to meet the demands of our followers, whose number was growing by the thousands every day. I no longer had time to administer advice in person, but instead, issued daily statements which were filmed and then broadcast worldwide on a satellite television network, as well as on the World Wide Web. Within a few years, I had once again become one of the wealthiest and most famous men in the world.

After a while, though, I realized that I had strayed far from my original quest, and decided that the only way to get back to what really mattered was to start from the beginning. I realized that I missed performing my Vaudeville act and selling life insurance.

So I bought a new Plymouth, almost identical to the first, packed it up with insurance forms and policies and maps, and headed out on the road again. I bought a new striped suit and squirting flower and began polishing my act. I learned new magic tricks, made up funnier jokes, and played several musical instruments, sometimes at once. My act grew so popular, I decided to hire an assistant. After a few months, we added a short Russian man who smoked huge cigars while performing tricks with a fat caged bear, and as more performers joined our act, we had to buy several large trucks and a tent. We had a bearded fat lady, two camels, an elephant, a family of tightrope walkers, and a lion tamer from Bolivia.

Our circus became the most popular in the world, with amazing tricks and acts, and me at the center of the ring directing it all. I was happy, living simply and humbly in my small circus trailer. And with time, I also had a small family, and they performed in the circus with me. We were all so happy and content: me, my three wives, and our twenty-seven children.

Over the years, I gained several hundred pounds, lost most of my hair, and began spending my days lounging in a custom-made, over-sized bed, but I was revered by all as a wise, patient, and loving old man. My family grew along with the circus as grandchildren, then great-grandchildren, then great-great-grandchildren were born. I became the patriarch of a vast, sprawling family of circus performers and entertainers around the world.

Finally, I felt that I had found my peace. I was doing what made me most happy. I was satisfied with my life, content, complete, fulfilled. I had achieved all my dreams. Life was wonderful. I no longer sought eternal existence. I no longer contemplated the meaning of existence, or my place in the universe. I didn't even think about the universe. I just was. I had reached nirvana. My whole existence was perfection. It was so good. I felt without a doubt that I was the luckiest human being alive. My life was a success.

Don Ferruco en la Alameda
su bastón quería tirar

Sollie's Letters

Sollie didn't need an alarm clock. Every morning at exactly 4:15, his eyes would flap open wide like one of those ventriloquist dummies and he would jump out of bed and start getting ready. He knew the East Coast and Wall Street were already humming with activity what with the time difference. He would wash his face and wet his graying hair. He had one white shirt, which he kept on a hanger next to his bed, and which he had owned for six years now. He had a pair of brown trousers and a matching coat with thin, worn leather patches on the elbows. These he hung from the curtain rod to make sure they got a little air every night. Sollie had a small yellow bow tie. All of these he put on with great care in front of his dirty mirror above the sink filled with greasy pots and plates and forks.

Once he was dressed, Sollie sat down to wipe his brown wingtips with an oily rag and water. The shoes were cracked and worn. The left shoe had a large hole in the sole, but Sollie just wrapped a few layers of toilet paper around his foot where the hole was. When his shoes were shined, he put them on, picked up his briefcase and small transistor radio, and stepped out into the pre-dawn street to catch the 5:45 Alameda bus downtown.

On the bus, Sollie would watch the other passengers. When he was sure someone had taken notice of him, he would set the radio down next to him, place the thin briefcase on his lap (making sure the side with the duct tape was facing down), open the briefcase, and pull out his copy of the Wall Street Journal. Over the years, it had begun to deteriorate and yellow at the edges, but Sollie took great care of his Wall Street Journal, and figured it could probably last him a few more years at least.

Sollie did not need glasses, but he had a pair he had stolen from a drugstore, and he would put these on with a grand gesture, clear his throat, lean back, and with a stern look on his face, begin to examine the letters and symbols on the pages. he would set his chin on his thumb and place his index finger on his lips in a thoughtful pose as he read over columns and rows of stock prices, highs and lows and changes, ticker tape symbols. He would nod once in a while, especially when he saw his audience was watching. Sometimes he would let out an exasperated grunt as if he had seen something particularly frustrating or annoying in all those rows and rows and columns of numbers and symbols.

When someone looked especially interested, Sollie might fold the paper and look at the person over his bifocals. "You read the Journal?" he would say, knowing from their appearance that they probably did not. When they affirmed his suspicions, he would shake his head. "That's a shame. You got to read the Journal. This is the key. See all them numbers. That's all you need to get rich. 's all these letters and numbers, man. If you understand them, you got it made. 's all there, plain as day." Then he would go back to looking at the numbers as if he were deciphering some deep, profound secret.

When the bus let him off at Figueroa and Exposition, he would fold the paper up again carefully and place it in his briefcase, then step out onto the street and begin his walk to school. He kept the radio tuned to NPR or AM radio talk shows for the latest financial information. The rest of the day, Sollie would wander around the campus of the university. Sometimes he talked to people, but most of the time, he talked to himself.

But he wasn't just talking to himself. He was delivering lectures on economic theory and financial analysis. To illustrate major points, he might pull out his Wall Street Journal and point to a number or line. When he saw the campus security guys coming, he would pick up the briefcase and radio and start walking fast the other direction.

"I got a lecture to give, that's all," he'd say.

"If we see you here bothering the kids again, we're gonna have to take you in Sollie," they would say, and he would feel the sweat building up on his forehead.

"I won't, I promise. I just got a lecture to give, that's all, I'm on my way," he'd say, wiping at the sweat with a ragged piece of tissue. They called him the Professor. Professor Sollie.

In the evenings, Sollie would take his briefcase and his radio to Barney's apartment. Barney lived alone, like him, and came from Louisiana, like him. They would talk about deep fried catfish and crawdad etouffé, and chicken gumbo, but mostly, they ate canned soup and beans and big yellow blocks of government-issued cheese.

Once a month, Sollie asked Barney to transcribe a letter for him. He said that a man of his intelligence and experience should not have to be burdened with writing letters himself. Barney always nodded and agreed profusely that he should act as Sollie's transcription secretary. Sollie's letters always said pretty much the same thing:

Dear Mom and Pop,

Life in Los Angeles is just dandy. I got myself a great job in the financial world just like I said I would, and I have been promoted several times. And I am a teacher too, just like you wanted mama. I give lectures to hundreds and thousands of students like on that movie we saw, remember? I am living a good life, but money is still a little tight so I won't be able to send anything until next month, but it will be a big stack of hundred dollar bills, I promise. I got some investments in the works and they'll come through any day now. Well that's it for now, take care and don't worry none about me.

Your loving son,

Sollie

Barney always agreed with Sollie that this was indeed a fine letter, and when Sollie asked him to read it back, he could just say it from memory because he had heard it so many times already. Sollie let Barney sign his name. He said it looked better to have it all in the same handwriting. Then they would fold the letter up carefully and put it in an envelope which Sollie had found at the school or on the street somewhere. In his pocket, Sollie carried a stained and heavily creased piece of paper which said:

Oliver and Mary Bloodsaw
3 Rue Carrolton
Monroe, LA 71202

Barney would copy the lines carefully, letter by letter, onto the envelope, and promise Sollie he would take it the post office later. But when Sollie left, Barney would throw the letter into his small closet with all the rest of them. He never sent any of them, because even though the letters looked real on the page and seemed to make up real words, they were really just little pictures and shapes he had learned to draw by copying dirty magazines and newspaper scraps.

When Barney died, Sollie found the closet full of letters—over two hundred of them piled against the back wall, along with dozens of dirty magazines. He filled a big plastic trash bag with the magazines and took them home.

El que le cantó a San Pedro,
no le volverá a cantar

Rooster

Maricela's truth is a dying rooster brought back to life with a cast iron pot and a wooden spoon. "You put the pot over the rooster," she says, "and then you bang the pot with a wooden spoon. Five times. You never heard of that?"

"No," I say. "Does it work?"

"Sometimes it works," she says.

Once, Maricela had a white and yellow cockteau named Tweety. He would walk around her apartment picking at the carpet for bugs and food. He could fly, but he liked to walk around like a dog or something, you know, and since he never tried to go outside the apartment, they left his cage door open so he could come and go whenever he wanted.

One day, Maricela's sister Vero stepped on Tweety by accident, that bitch. Everybody heard the bird scream and Maricela ran and found Tweety all shuddering and twisting his neck on the hallway floor. Vero said, "Sorry," and walked into her room, like nothing had happened.

"So I picked up Tweety and took him to my dad, all crying." He put the bird under a small iron pot, and then he banged the pot five times, really loud, with an old wooden spoon, you know, those big ones, and she it's not going to work it's not going to work pinche Vero and he watch your mouth, look, stop crying, he's going to be okay, see, and lifting the pot, Tweety jumping out as good as new and running around the living room floor. He even jumped up onto the coffee table.

But a few days later, Tweety was sitting on the perch in his cage when he started leaning forward really slow. All of a sudden, he just fell.

"I was sitting there watching TV, and I saw him leaning forward like out of the corner of my eye, you know, and then I just hear him fall like with a thud sound." She lets the back of one hand fall heavily into the palm of the other. He was dead. This time, the pot and spoon didn't work.

I'm really good at lying. I'm so good, my whole family thinks I can't keep a secret or tell a lie. Did you think I was such a good liar? I know, nobody imagines, because I'm small and innocent-looking and I'm so good at it. You know what I do? Sometimes out of the blue, I'll say something like, "Servando, remember I told you how I lent Frank five bucks for lunch the other day?" but I know I didn't tell him that before. I just know how much it bugs him that I lend Frank money, and of course, he gets all mad and says, "No, you didn't tell me," and I say, "Oops, I didn't?" and act all stupid like I let it slip out, and he says, "Man, you can't hold water," and my whole family tells me the same thing, that I can't keep a secret to save my life. But that's what I want them to say, so that when I really tell them lies, they believe me because they think I'm so bad at telling lies that I must be telling the truth. That's bad, ha? God, I can't believe I told you that. Now you'll never believe me. But I promise, I won't lie to you. You'll be my clean friend, okay? All my other friends, I lied to here and there, not big lies, just not always the whole truth, I've dirtied myself with them, you know? But I'll start clean with you and tell you everything with no lies, okay? I need a clean friend. See, you already know about my lying, and nobody knows that, so I can't lie to you now, right?

Maricela believes in the Bible. She used to carry around a copy of the New Testament with her. I don't know if she still does. I remember when I first saw the little red book in her purse. I said, "Where's the rest of it?"

She said, "The rest of what?"

"The Bible," I said. "Where's the Old Testament?"

She clicked her teeth with her tongue. "Shut up. You don't even believe in the Bible anyway. What do you care?"

"I was just curious, that's all. And I never really said I don't believe-I just don't know," I said. I flipped through the small gold-trimmed pages of the book. "You know, I think there was a Jesus and he was an okay guy, but I think maybe he was just a military revolutionary, you know, not necessarily the son of God."

"Anyway. Give me back my book. You're making me mad," she said.

"No, seriously, there's a lot of documented proof that supports the theory of Jesus as a military leader." I was only half serious in pressing the issue, because I knew she would never believe me.

"No, seriously, give me back my book." I could see she was upset, so I handed her the book and dropped the subject.

After a while, she said, "I carry this with me for comfort."

"I know," I said. "I'm sorry."

Servando is so dark, moreno pero moreno de Zacatecas, and well, we both have a lot of dark hair, you know? I mean, not just on our heads. So I was so afraid the baby would come out a little monkey. Servando's mom said he looked like a little mono when he came out, so I thought, oh my god, we're going to have a little monkey baby. Sure enough, she came out so dark pero morenita Rubén, and with a full head of black black hair, and hair on her back and arms even. But she was so beautiful. We were so happy, you know? And that day, Sunday, México won the World Cup. I tried to call you from the hospital to tell you and to tell you happy birthday-can you believe she was born on your birthday?-but nobody answered. That's okay, though. There was already a bunch of people packed into that tiny hospital room-I couldn't believe how many people came, you know? It was so nice, and the nurses even let them all stay for a little while even though we were already way over the limit for visitors. It was so nice.

Patmos is a nice place to die I think. It is warm and quiet here. I sit on the sand and listen to the calm sea which surrounds my island and stretches into nothing on all sides. I watch my six chickens and my rooster in the small wooden pen I built for them. There is time to think, and remember, and I sit and think and write these scrolls and seal them in clay jars so that after I am gone, maybe there will be some record of the truth left. Nobody bothers with an old man like me, nobody cares, and that is just fine with me. I like the peace.

I bury the jars with my scrolls in the ground of a cave away from the sea. But before I write each story, I tell it to myself over and over until I think I have remembered every detail, every word exactly as it was said...but even then, I know there will always be things changed or forgotten, or even things remembered which never really happened. I once tried to write a detailed account of everything that happened, as did the others, but one by one, he changed our stories to fit his own, until the only truth they held was the truth Paul preached, and it was as if nothing that I remembered had really happened.

Since then, I think a lot about the truth. I think, even if I do write this down, even if it is read centuries from now, it will still be only a hollow shell of the real story of what happened, because it is just my story. And, if people choose to believe Paul's story instead, well then, indeed, with time, that will very well become the truth, as true as anything that really did happen. Why not? When we are dust, the truth will be dust with us, and there will be only the ever-changing truth of time and circumstance. And who knows, maybe Paul's truth will work even better than the real truth as I know it anyway. Maybe the real truth was never meant to stand the test of time as well as Paul's truth.

But some mornings when my rooster crows, I think of Peter, and I remember the real truth. It is true that he denied him, but the story of the rooster crowing on the third betrayal was Paul's, and it was not true. I remember they asked him if he was one of the zealot-bandits, and he denied it, just as we had planned from the beginning, and they then why are you called Peter the Zealot and Peter the Rooster? Is it not because of your fierce skills as a warrior for the movement and he I have never heard those names, I do not know their origins. I am no warrior. I am just a fisherman. That is the truth. That is the truth exactly as I remember it...well, almost; I think there was a girl, too, a servant girl, but I cannot remember clearly...let me see...she loved Peter, I think, yes...no, that's not it, I think...

In any case, I was there. Paul was not.

Sometimes, when I grow bored with the silence and with my scattered memories, I make up fantastic stories of strange visions and terrible beasts, and I read them, out loud...to my chickens. I think they like my stories. They are chickens, anyway. They don't care so much if I tell them the truth, or forget a few details here and there; they are happy with a good story, so I give them one.

I still sometimes ask God for the truth. I say to Him, were we not fiery warriors, ready to die in Your name, to do anything to restore Your promised kingdom of David? Did he not call me and my brother 'Sons of Thunder?' *(here I pound my chest, several times, muttering 'Sons of Thunder,' then roaring it in the direction of my chickens and watching them scatter, clucking and squawking nervously)*...did we not follow Your word, even when we saw that he was not really the Messiah, but merely a man like the rest of us? *(I raise both hands to the sky, imploringly, pathetically)*...we shed our blood for You, we hid like thieves in the night, we slit the throats of Roman soldiers, and plotted bloody revolution in Your name. What did we do wrong? What did we do to deserve this end, this pathetic exile worse than anything we had even before we tried to win our freedom? *(this is where the tears begin to stream down my cheeks, and I touch my fingers to my wet face in mock surprise)*...what did we do wrong?

But all I hear are the chickens clucking like fools at one another, fighting over worms in the ground, and I wonder how the voice of a tired old man sounds to His ears.

When we took her home, it was really cold and windy outside, but we kept her all bundled up and covered with blankets. Everybody was waiting for us in the driveway, my dad had a video camera and he filmed us driving up and getting out of the car. We got her into the house quick and the dogs were all running around with all the excitement and everything. You know how chihuahuas are. Muñequa kept jumping up and down off the couch and running back and forth from the living room to the bedroom where we put her crib next to our bed. Everything was okay, but she wouldn't eat. I tried to breast feed her, then I pumped milk with the machine, and nothing. She wouldn't eat. But, it wasn't like she was fussy or something. She would just lay there with the nipple in her mouth and she wouldn't suck on it, like she didn't care. So I called the hospital and they said, "Is this your first baby?" like I didn't know what I was doing, and I said, "Yes, but something just seems wrong," and the nurse said, "Well, it's normal. Don't worry. Wait a few hours, let her sleep. She's probably tired." So I said okay and hung up and we waited, but she wouldn't eat, still. We started getting really worried, so I called the hospital again and told them to page my doctor. It was already late, and he was at home, but he called back and I told him she wouldn't eat, and still, he said it was normal and not to worry even though it was already like seven hours since we brought her home. He said he didn't think anything was wrong, but that if we really felt like anything was wrong, we should take her to the hospital right away. So we said okay again, and hung up. Servando called his brother Beto and told him we were worried, and he said that wasn't right, she should have eaten by now. Beto has seven kids, so he knows about babies. He said he would come right over. When he got there, she still wouldn't eat, and she had turned like a purple color.

"Has he ever cheated on you?"

"No, not really," she says, "But one time, he kind of lied about some girl he met."

"What do you mean?"

"Well, see, I got him a pager, just so he could have one, you know? Not because I was trying to keep track of him or anything, but just because, you know?"

So anyway, she would always tell him to go out with his friend George, dancing, whatever. He would never go out, always there in the house, sentado in front of the TV. But finally one night he went out dancing, who knows why. The next day, he was outside, fixing the car or something, you know, and he gets a page. The pager was on the kitchen table, but she didn't look at it-why would she look at it, you know?

"I would never suspect anything," she says. "I just took it outside to him without looking at it." And he couldn't even play it off. He looks at the number all like nervous and weird, right? And he says she can't lie.

So anyway, she went into the house and watched him through the window, and she he's so stupid Rubén, he goes upstairs to my mom's apartment to call from there. So obvious, you know?

"But I didn't say anything. I just acted like nothing happened," she says, and I nod. "A few days later, he left his pager at home, and he got another page, so I memorized the number."

I laugh. "You memorized the number?"

Yes, she memorized the number, but again, she didn't say anything; she just acted like nothing happened. Then about a week or so later, again, another page comes in with the same number. So she called the number.

"I saw it was the same number as before, some 818 number, so I called it," she says.

"And a girl answered..." I say.

And a girl answered, of course. Bitch. She said, "'Uh, did somebody page?'"

"And the girl said, 'Yeah, I did,' and I said, 'Well, he's not here right now. What did you need?'" And the girl he ordered some Avon (or something) and his order had come in and this and this and that and Maricela bitch shut the fuck up, yeah right, why would he order Avon? Stupid puta.

"So later on, I confronted him, and he broke down and said it was just some girl he met when they went dancing.

"'But why did you give her your pager number?'

"'Just.'

"Anyway. Then he really broke down and said he was sorry and nothing had happened and he wouldn't do it again.

"'I'm sorry, really, nothing happened.'"

"So what did you say?" I say.

"I said, 'Okay,' but I told him that if he was going to be lying to me, at least lie good and don't get caught. 'If you're going to tell lies, at least do it good. Don't get caught.'

"That way, if I never know the real truth, then it's like it never happened. I mean, if you think about it, it kind of never did happen then, really, if I don't know about it, you know?"

I nod and hear her say again that she doesn't care so much if he lies, just as long as he doesn't get caught, but my mind has become a little dazed and lost in trying to follow all these twists in the way she tells her story, and sensing this, she tries to change the subject.

"Hey, you know what? Nobody ever sees my feet," she says. "I don't let anybody see my feet." Trying to picture her small, hidden feet brings me somewhat back to reality, to the present, and I look down at her black work boots.

"Why not?"

"Well, I...well, okay, look: last night, I went to Pic 'n Save and bought my first pair of sandals. Ever." She sighs deeply and looks at me with wide brown eyes as if she has just revealed something profound, momentous, and frightening. I shake my head and look down at her boots, then back up at her with a look of concern etched into my face.

"And are you sure you're okay with this decision to wear sandals? I mean, it is a big step for such small feet."

"I don't know," she says, and I can see that she is taking my question very seriously. "I think, 'I'm never going to wear these.' And you know I've had huaraches before, but even with those, I wore thick socks. I always wear at least two pairs of socks all the time. See?" She rolls up her pant leg and peels away three layers of thick white wool socks above her left boot.

"But it's just your feet," I hear myself say, but again, I am distracted from the conversation, this time in trying to imagine her feet. I know they are small, but, are the toes small and stubby too, or long and finger-like? And are the nails painted red, or just clipped short and even and left uncolored? I wonder if all this obsessive covering has left her feet pale, translucent, and I imagine the pattern left on them by her socks, and little bits of cotton material from the socks stuck here and there between sweaty toes, or in the waffle design etched into her skin by the pattern of the cloth. And I wonder if her feet are crossed with thin, blue, snake-like veins, or if they are thick and fleshy with no veins touching the surface at all.

Are you laughing at me? I hear her say. "Are you laughing at me?" she says.

"No...I...it's just your feet, you know?" Are the soles hard and callused, or soft and fleshy from always being covered?

She says, "No, see, to me, my feet are like another private part of my body, you know? I don't like to let anybody see them. They're my feet."

Immediately, I feel my face turning red at having tried to imagine them, these suddenly private parts of her body. I say, "Okay, I guess I understand," but I shake my head and smile as if I don't.

I do see, though, but I do not admit it, for fear of acknowledging too much that might make us both uncomfortable. I think she senses this.

"Anyway," she says, "Why am I telling you this?" and walks away, on her feet.

...we're going to see the roosters fight mi 'jo where's my mama I'm taking you, your mama's staying here to learn how to make tortillas with the Mexican ladies, I'm going with daddy okay he's happy, daddy's not mad that lady scared me daddy, that lady on the hill, I know mi 'jo, that high hill with the old rusty cars at the bottom and the sky smells like pepper and pee, she was a witch, a bruja mi 'jo, but she was a good witch and she said you'll be big and strong, but she scared me and I cried, where's my mama, come on, let's go see the roosters, aren't you excited, smile (smile) excited okay yeah the roosters, you smell like beer daddy, why are you so quiet mi 'jo I don't know where are the roosters, you'll see, so many people everywhere, so many legs all around in the night it's so dark no lights on the street, I can't understand them nobody speaks English here daddy where are you I'm right here mi 'jo hold my hand don't get lost I'm scared look, mira, mira los roosters mi 'jo, look at the roosters, way down there everybody yelling money in tight fists in the air mira los gallos mi 'jo, you like the roosters (shake head) yes smile (smile) scared eyes smell beer it's so dark in here the wood bench is damp and moist hands paper cups on the ground hot sticky air the roosters fly into the air and crash into each other, screeching, feathers everywhere, then the men pull them back and everybody standing up yelling and then again the roosters in the air I can't see daddy I have to pee I have to pee the roosters scare me like the witch like the scorpion I poked with a stick and you came running down and pushed

it away with your boot like you like okay let's go nobody sees me down here in the dark where's the bathroom I pee by myself because I am a big boy and the air smells like pee and caca and everybody is so dark and when I am done I pull my pants up I look around and feel my eyes get big daddy DADDY where are you my heart stops looking around at belt buckles and boots for yours daddy and everybody is looking at me at this little white boy little huerito lost in the bathroom with big scared eyes run out into the dark street into a bigger forest of more strange legs and belts and buckles with scorpions and bull horns daddy feel the tears coming up where are you all these people speaking Spanish all the strangers everything is dark in the street I smell pee and beer and cigarettes start to cry I'm so scared mama daddy grandma Kristy Uncle Andrew Auntie Penny Uncle Paul Auntie Sandy Uncle Peter Tío Juan just like the song just like the Beatles song somebody's knockin' on the door somebody's ringin' the bell somebody's knockin' on the...somebody's...ringin'...somebodysomedbody's... somebody's somebo.........where ARE you I'm so scared daddy I'm so scared daddy this scares me like the roosters like the scorpion like the witch like you like you daddy like you lift me up from behind suddenly and I can see over a wobbling sea of cowboy hats and I am too terrified to scream and I know my heart will not start again until I recognize your rough hands under my thin arms and your smell and then I'm not so scared anymore (I think) but the fear is still there the fear is still there the fear is still there with you daddy and you say, here's my gallo catchetón and smile and lift me in the air higher and I (smile) but the fear is still there daddy the fear is still there daddy the fear is still there in my heart with you, dad...

Maricela's brother-in-law, Beto, fights roosters. Once, he had a beautiful rooster named Chincho. It was his favorite, all shiny red and brown and white with bright black eyes and thick claws. He always won *(have you ever been to a rooster fight? once, I say, but I was very little and don't remember it very well...it was in México)*, and anyway, one day, while Beto was gone, Maricela noticed that Chincho was walking weird, all slow and crooked. She called her dad and he looking at the bird I think it's sick. They tried to nurse it back to health with a humidifier and blankets and castor oil, but within a few hours, the bird could not even walk, and just sat there all quiet, his eyes all droopy, until they just closed and he fell over. Servando put a pot over him and banged it five times, with a spoon*(of course)*, and when they took the pot away, the bird ran out into the yard.

"But when Beto came home, Chincho was all weird again, walking slow and all chuecked out like he was going to fall over again, until he did right in the middle of the driveway. We tried everything. Beto held him in his lap and spit into his face and then rubbed the spit into his feathers, but Chincho wouldn't get up. We tried the pot again, but it didn't work. Beto just started crying and crying and petting Chincho, rubbing his feathers and blowing into his beak. He loved that bird, you know?"

All night, Beto sat there on the couch with Chincho in his lap, just crying and rubbing the bird's feathers, and they Beto he's dead come to bed and he leave me alone and shaking his head rubbing the bird and they silent not knowing what to do until her dad come on mi 'ja let's leave him alone now whispering and leading her away and he still silent and crying there on the couch with the dead bird in his lap and they found him like that still the next morning, and when we *got to the hospital, she was really purple already. At first, the doctor took the bottle like he was going to show me how to do it right, but then he saw how she was and they rushed her into the emergency room. She went into cardiac arrest, but they brought her back. A nurse came out and said we could keep her there and try to save her, but her chances were not good unless we got her to the pediatric specialty center in Orange County.*

"It was like a dream, where things happen really fast, you know," and suddenly you're somewhere *different from a second ago and everything is the same but all changed*somehow. *I mean, we were still in the same hospital, but now it was a different hospital, because just a second ago, in the first hospital, I had a baby. In this new hospital, all of sudden, I knew I might never have her again.* Then the nurse was a doctor, but she *didn't see her change into the doctor. He said she had a better chance at Children's Hospital because they had the best equipment and specialists there, but there was a risk she might go into cardiac arrest again in the ambulance. We decided to take the chance, so they rushed her there in the ambulance and we followed them in our car, Servando drove. The whole drive wasn't real-it was like it didn't happen. I mean, I know it happened, because then suddenly we were in Orange County at the other hospital, but I can't* *remember any of it, and I still feel like it didn't happen. At the other hospital, they hooked her up in the emergency room and she went into cardiac arrest again. We were in the waiting room, but we could hear everything, I could h*ear when Pilate went into the palace and called Jesus. 'Are you the King of the Jews?' he asked him.

... 'No, my kingdom does not belong here!'

So Pilate asked him, 'Are you a king, then?'

Jesus answered, 'You say that I am a king. I was born and came into the world for this one purpose, to speak about the truth. Whoever belongs to the truth listens to me.'

'And what is the truth?' Pilate asked," and w*e could hear the little beep on the heartbeat machine stop. She was in cardiac arrest for thirty minutes before they brought her back again. They kept working, but again, we heard the beep stop for the third time and then finally the doctor came out and asked us if we wanted the priest to come and we said yes and he came and read the last rites and then they do you want to go in and see her one last time and we yes and we went in and oh my god Rubén, she was so small on the table, all purple, she was so purple, like one big bruise, like a big bruised purple pear, all covered with hair, and there was a million wires sticking out of her, all over, sticking out of her mouth and her ears and her nose and her belly button, red and white and green and blue and yellow wires and tubes, and she looked so still, like she was just one more little purple part of all the big machines, and the lights, and the wires, all around her, and we just stood there looking at her, and she was dead, just like that, like she had never even been born, like* *all those nine months and everything had never happened.*

But I knew it had happened, I knew it had all happened, because I could see her there on the table, not moving, and all I could think was that God was finally punishing me. He was taking her away, even after everything the doctors had tried, because He knew my secret, He knew the truth. I couldn't lie to Him, no matter how good I was at it, because He already knew all my secrets, and all the truth, and now she's just there, on the table, all tiny, and purple, and dead.

ACKNOWLEDGMENTS

I wish to thank my family and friends for their support.

Also, special thanks to Elizabertha Gastelum for helping to keep me sheltered and fed while writing most of this.

And to Jim Kincaid, whose direction, encouragement, and belief in me have proven invaluable, my deepest gratitude.